I0598990

Copyright © 2022 by Jessica Babcock

First paperback edition July 3, 2022

Book design by Roger Broussard

ISBN 978-1-7374720-0-1 (paperback)
ISBN 978-1-7374720-1-8 (ebook)

www.jessicababcock.com

Chapter 1

Awakening from a light sleep by snapping twigs, he reached for his sword, cursing softly as his sword slipped from the sheath and fell to the ground beside him. Strong fingers finding the sword, he gripped it tightly, lying close to the damp earth. The first light of early morning was filtering through the thick canopy of trees casting shadows through the mist that blanketed the deep green foliage. As he looked through the branches of the thicket, the shadows moved. He tightened the grip on his sword with tensed muscles before he made out the form of a doe with her fawn. Still, he crouched, listening—waiting. He was almost there; he could not fail now.

Stepping from the thick foliage he considered the distance and caught sight of Nottes Castle. It loomed like a sleeping giant in the cool misty morning. The first rays of the morning sun were starting to wash over the gray stones. The tall towers casting a smoky shadow on the dewy green hillside. He paused letting the rays of the sun warm his body, his sore muscles starting to release the tension they held for the last few days during his trip to the castle.

He pulled the hood of his cloak over his head walking toward the brook. The brook babbled as it wound its way around the base of the hill and disappeared into the thick woods that surrounded the outer castle grounds. The hill was steep and rocky except for one side that was covered with thick green grass. The hill and brook were perfect protection for the castle. With nothing around for miles except dense forests and wild animals, it was a haven for all who were welcomed.

He walked through the village toward the outer castle wall. Most of the villagers gave him little notice. A large man shoeing a horse stopped and watched as he walked by. The open fire pit heating the metal glowing like a red eye in the darkness of the shop. A man walked up to the blacksmith with a horse. The two men spoke for a moment, then went about their business.

As he approached the outer castle wall, he heard the large drawbridge groan from being lowered. The hooves of horses heard on the wooden bridge. A knight on horseback approached him.

"Welcome, Lord Elwyn." The knight pulled on the reins of his horse, dropping the reins of another horse that followed within reach of Aethelhard's hands. He reached for the reins and gave a quick look toward the forest. The knight's eyes following, grasping his sword's handle. "Were you followed?"

Aethelhard mounted the horse and started to turn him toward the bridge that separated him from safety. "Not that I'm aware."

As if sensing danger, the horses' quick strides were soon heard on the wooden bridge. The groan of the large chains lifting the heavy bridge started before the horses were over the bridge. Aethelhard breathed deeply, bowing his head for his safe journey to the castle.

His head lifting as they approached the stables. "Has my steed arrived?"

"Yes, milord. The woman brought your steed to the castle early last eve. She was paid in gold coins as requested and left soon after." The knight dismounted his horse, handing the reins to a waiting stable boy.

Aethelhard dismounted and walked toward the stable. "Good. I was hoping I could trust her. There are many in the Kingdom I can no longer trust."

If I may say, I have not seen a steed as magnificent as yours before," spoke the knight.

"He cost me a small bag of gold coins, but he was worth it," Aethelhard said. He walked to a stable boy who had finished grooming one of the horses. "Where is the steed that came last eve?"

The boy looked to Aethelhard then to the knight who nodded his approval. "In here, milord." He led the horse he was grooming into a stable stall. Then stopped by the second stall.

The steed's hooves pawed at the ground and Aethelhard reached over the sturdy boards to run his hand over his muzzle. "He seems to have made the journey quite well." He looked through the slats to see if there were any obvious injuries to his steed.

"Yes, milord. Lord D'arcy checked the steed after the woman brought him. He made sure he was not sick or injured before paying her. I groomed him late last eve after his arrival."

Lord Elwyn set his heavy boot on the slat and patted the steed's neck. "You have done well. My steed is content."

The boy smiled for a moment at the rare compliment.

"Ah, Aethelhard. I thought you might be here," Lord Hutton D'arcy said as he rounded the corner and walked into the stable. "That's one fine steed you have. Come. Let's go to the dining hall. Breakfast was being set on the table as you arrived." Hutton led him away from the stables and toward the ramp that led to another drawbridge. As they walked over the bridge, Aethelhard saw the men working on an abatis in the deep trench that separated the lower bailey from the upper bailey. "Why the additional fortification, Hutton? Expecting a siege on your own lands?"

"Only a precaution. The lands have grown dangerous all over, as I'm sure you found out during your journey here. I'm glad to see you made it alive."

They approached the dining hall and Aethelhard breathed deeply of the fragrant air. It smelled of fresh baked bread and sausages. "I am as well. Tonight, will be my first good sleep since I left the castle."

"Sit down. Kylin can finish her mead in the solar with her mother."

Kylin turned her head hearing the two approaching. On seeing Aethelhard and her father, she spoke softly, her eyes lingering for only a moment on Aethelhard. "Yes, Father."

Aethelhard bowed. "Good morning, Kylin."

Kylin nodded. "Good morning, Aethelhard." He heard the soft rustle of her dress as she stepped quietly out of the dining hall.

Hutton sat down as a servant brought out a pitcher of mead along with plates of biscuits and sausages. They sat quietly for a few minutes. Hutton drank his mead as Aethelhard finished his plate of biscuits and sausages. "Where did you buy that fine steed?" Hutton said finally breaking the silence.

Aethelhard poured another cup of mead. "I got him at a public sale in a nearby village. I knew as soon as I saw him, he was perfect."

"Must have cost you a bag of gold to get him." Hutton leaned back in his chair.

Aethelhard drank his mead for a moment. "Yes, he did. Wouldn't have cost me as much except for a man who kept bidding against me. He looked as if he might be a knight." Aethelhard paused, taking another sip of mead. "I'm not sure how a knight would have that much gold unless he was a rogue."

"Did you recognize him?"

"No, but I was in a village I had not been through before."

Hutton leaned forward setting his cup on the worn wooden table. "Do you remember the name of the village?"

Hutton turned his head hearing a soft rustle from the doorway. "Yes, Kylin?"

"I'm sorry to disturb you, father, but mother wishes to see you in the solar. She said it was important."

Hutton shook his head lightly as he stood. "Excuse me. I'll be back in a few minutes. Kylin, would you keep Aethelhard company while I'm away?"

"Yes, father," Kylin said. She sat across from him refilling her cup with mead.

"It's been a long time since I've seen you," Aethelhard said as he looked over her. She'd grown into a beautiful woman over the last few years. He thought back to their childhood years when they ran through the meadows and he showed her a toad he caught. A smile tugged on the corners of his mouth remembering the horrified look her mother had when she proudly showed her the toad.

"It's been a long time since you've visited the castle," Kylin said. She brought the mead cup to her lips taking a sip before setting it down. "I've not been able to leave the castle even with my attendants and knights these last few months because of the danger."

"I'm sorry that I couldn't visit sooner but there have been responsibilities at my own castle that kept me away. Even now my visit is for business." Aethelhard took another drink of his mead, his eyes looking over her lithe form. He took a deep breath wishing it were not so; that he could visit with her. But matters of the castle took precedence and it was his experience that women only complicated matters.

"I've heard about the unrest on your land. Of course, father does not talk about such things when I'm in the room." She watched as his eyes drank her in, a soft smile on her lips.

Aethelhard shifted uneasy in his chair. "Your father is right. This is not an area that a woman should concern herself. Your concern is running the castle, not protecting it."

Hutton walked back into the hall and stood beside Kylin. His face was stern. "You may join your mother in the solar. I will talk with you later."

Kylin stood, her eyes lowering for a moment, her cheeks flushing lightly. "Yes, father." She turned and left the room.

"Is something wrong?" Aethelhard watched as Kylin left the room and Hutton started to pace in front of the large hearth.

Hutton clasped his hands behind him thoughtfully. He looked toward the door, then back to Aethelhard. "I'm not sure what to do with Kylin."

"What do you mean?" Aethelhard said with concern. Everything appeared to be fine only a few moments ago when he talked with her.

Hutton took a deep breath and continued to pace before the hearth. "Kylin has turned down another suitor. I'm at a loss as to what to do with her. She's convinced her mother that she would be miserable with him." He waved his hand as if to dismiss his problems. "We need to get back to the more pressing matters at hand. Why the sudden visit to my castle? I had thought you would be busy with your father calming the unrest at your castle."

Aethelhard shifted once more in his chair and watched the flames in the hearth, dance and lick at the dry bark surrounding the large log. A small wisp of gray smoke forming over the log, swirling, and finally spiraling toward the flue. His fingers moved lightly over the blood on his breeches. He grew quiet, reflecting on his last moments in the castle. "I no longer have control over the castle," he said quietly.

"Blackmon took control of the castle?" Hutton looked at him in disbelief.

"Yes." Aethelhard moved uneasy in his chair, the recent wound on his thigh burning like a hot coal in the hearth.

Hutton noticed the grimace on his face as he shifted. "Were you wounded in the battle?"

"An arrow glanced off my leg as I was escaping through the forest." Aethelhard stared into the hearth watching the glowing coals. "I need your help. The castle has fallen into enemy hands. There are traitors in the castle. I don't know who I can trust anymore."

Hutton nodded. "I heard rumors the castle had fallen to Blackmon." Hutton poured another cup of mead from the pitcher sitting on the table. "What about your father? Why is he not here? It's his castle."

"Not anymore," Aethelhard said, his eyes still looking deep into the flames of the hearth.

Hutton sat down across from him. "What happened?"

"Blackmon's men killed him. I saw his head on a pole above the castle walls." Aethelhard's hands trembled causing the mead to slosh in his cup, his face becoming tense.

"I'm sorry. Your father was a good friend." Hutton looked toward the door then back to Aethelhard.

Aethelhard took a deep breath trying hard to hold onto what little composure he had left. "Why do you think I'm here? I need your help. My father died defending his land." His face became angry. "Every insult they gave to my family is only more salt on an open wound. I must have my revenge!"

Hutton leaned toward him, his voice calm "Do not let your revenge be that which kills you," he said. There was silence as Hutton looked to the flames in the hearth. "I'm not sure I have that many men to spare. There's unrest along the border with Scotland again."

"I know. I tried to reach the King just before the siege of Elwyn Castle. I was told he was defending the English border against Scotland." Aethelhard slammed his cup on the table and watched the dark mead running over the surface of the table. It reminded him of his father's blood as it spilled on the slate floor in his last moments. "Are you going to help me or not? We do have an alliance."

"I had an alliance with your father," Hutton spoke calmly.

"He's dead," Aethelhard quickly stood as his chair crashed to the stone floor. "Are you going to honor the alliance with his son or not?"

Hutton contemplated the situation for a few minutes taking a deep breath. "It will be risky. Especially with so many of my men with the King."

"I'm asking for your help in taking back my father's land. Land that was taken from him just as yours will be if we don't stop Blackmon."

Hutton's fingers gripped the cup tightly as he looked to the wall that held the family coat of arms. At the bottom was the word 'Honor' was burned into the wood. He closed his eyes accepting the current alliance. "All right. I'll help based on the friendship and alliance I had with your father. But remember you are young. There is much you don't know and much that you must learn quickly. I'll be watching closely"

Aethelhard sat down, folding his hands on the table. "Thank you."

A servant walked in and replaced the pitcher of mead taking the empty pitcher with him. He started to clear the dishes from the table.

Hutton leaned back in his chair watching Geary clearing the table. "There's been much unrest lately. Your castle is not the only one to fall into enemy hands. With my men fighting battles in various places, my resources are limited."

"At least you know your men are loyal."

"Perhaps," Hutton took another drink of his mead. "But men's loyalties lie within the gold to pay them and their sense of victory. If they lose either, they'll go to those who have the gold and power. This recent unrest may only be the beginning of a larger battle."

"What do you mean?" Aethelhard said.

"This could be the start of another war. Scotland to the north has been engaging in many battles. Most of these battles have been over control of land." Hutton said his eyes slowly drifting to Geary. "That'll be all." Geary hurried his work taking the stack of dishes to the kitchen.

Aethelhard's fingers gripped the cup tighter, his patience worn thin. "How's that different from what has gone on for years? The strong always try to conquer those they perceive as weak."

"Yes, but this seems to be more than the usual skirmish over boundaries. Every country has a bottom to their gold and men to fight. But Scotland has been in constant battle for many years now. Yet, they still seem to have plenty of gold to pay their men and more men to replace those who perished."

Aethelhard looked at him for a moment. "Are we here to take back my father's land or to go on about something that may not even exist?"

"Perhaps both, but let's tend to your matter first. Tell me what your father told you about the castle's defenses and the current state of the land," Hutton said.

"The village outside the curtain wall was left mostly intact. Blackmon only burned the property of those he knew were loyal to my family or who might cause him problems. He killed the families as a warning to others in the village."

"How did Blackmon get into the castle?" Hutton shifted in the large wooden chair.

"Someone let him, and his men enter over the drawbridge and into the inner bailey. I heard the drawbridge lower as the siege on the castle started."

"Are you sure it was a traitor?"

Aethelhard shook his head. "It had to be a traitor. The soldiers guarding the drawbridge were loyal to my family."

Hutton looked to Aethelhard, deciding not to press the matter any further. "Any idea who let them in?"

"No. Blackmon must have been planning the attack on the castle for weeks. He had surrounded the land and cut off all our supplies. Food and water were dwindling rapidly."

Hutton nodded. "How did you escape?"

"Through a covered allure. It was built as a secret way out of the castle in case of attack. It leads to a tunnel that runs underground. The tunnel emerges at the edge of the village. From there, the forest is only a few steps away," Aethelhard said.

"The enemy soldiers did not see you emerging from the tunnel?" Hutton said remembering his wound.

"The soldiers caught up with me in the forest. I don't think they saw me emerging from the tunnel." Aethelhard's eyes became distant the images playing once more through his head.

Hutton looked to Aethelhard's leg. He saw the torn material of his breeches and the stain of dried blood. "Are there any other covered allures in the walls?"

"None that I know of…but there could be. Father hadn't told me of all the castle's secrets before he died."

"What other defenses does the castle have?"

"There is an outer curtain wall that goes around the castle, but care must be taken. There are many traps to catch those who get too close to the walls."

"Such as?" Hutton shifted in his chair.

"There are abatis and loops with oillets," Aethelhard said.

Hutton nodded, "Not a pleasant way to die but effective."

"What about the abatis I saw your men building? I'm sure there are other traps surrounding your castle as well," Aethelhard said nodding his head toward the inner drawbridge.

"Yes, a necessary evil," Hutton said.

Aethelhard continued. "There are three walls that must be breached before anyone can reach the keep. I'm sure Blackmon is staying there because of the fortification."

Hutton nodded. "Probably."

"The last wall is at the top of a steep rocky incline. This wall contains embrasures and machicolation for defending the high castle."

Hutton thought for a moment. "Where exactly does the covered allure start and the underground tunnel end?"

"There's a door in the wall that turns if pushed correctly. This is the entrance to the secret passage," Aethelhard said. "Once in the allure, you follow it through the castle walls to the steps that lead underground."

Hutton nodded. "And the tunnel ends just outside the village?"

"Yes," Aethelhard said. "If we use the secret passage, we must be careful. Blackmon may have already discovered it and be in wait for anyone using it."

Hutton thought for a moment drumming his fingers on his cup. "You know the defenses of the castle. This will be our advantage. But Blackmon could be adding other defenses just as I am increasing my fortification."

"Not in this brief period of time," Aethelhard said.

"Maybe, maybe not. But that's not a chance that I'm willing to take." He looked to Aethelhard and leaned closer to him, his eyes watching closely. "Are you?" Hutton paused letting the words sink in before he continued. "Did you notice anything about the land as you escaped into the forest?"

"How could I?" Aethelhard said. "I was escaping with my life."

"Even during escape, you should be observant of what is around you."

"What do you mean?" Aethelhard said his anger becoming evident.

"You must learn and memorize all the features of the land if you are to fight a battle and win. I've been to the castle many times to visit your father. There is a large rock with a dip in the land between the forest and the rock."

"That's right," Aethelhard said slowly.

Hutton stood. "You must remember everything about the land surrounding the castle. Even things you do not think are important can make the difference between victory or defeat…escape or dying." He looked toward the door, then back to Aethelhard. "I know you are tired from your journey. We'll talk later this eve after you've rested."

"Yes," Aethelhard said as he stood.

"The servants will help you with anything you need." Hutton walked toward the door leading out of the dining hall. "If you'll excuse me, I must attend to a personal matter with my daughter."

Aethelhard entered his chamber where he usually stayed while visiting the castle. In the center against the far wall was a large bed with a simple canopy and ornate carvings over the wooden posts. He tossed his cloak on a nearby chair, walking to the window, looking over the lake just beyond the castle grounds. His eyes drifted to the garden and the stone benches spread about where one could sit and enjoy the garden.

He reached into his pouch pulling out a worn map of his castle grounds and sat down at the small table. He carefully looked over the map, marking the spot where the large rock was located. How could he not remember that spot? What else had he overlooked that could help him? He ran his fingers roughly through his hair. He had to remember everything he could about the castle and the surrounding land. Anything, no matter how small, could be the turning point of the siege. There could be no mistakes. Blackmon would be waiting for him knowing he would return. But the more he looked at the map, the more muddled his mind became.

There was a soft knock on the door. "Yes?" Frustration evident in his voice.

"Milord D'arcy wanted to see if there was anything, I could get for you." The servant gently pushed open the door. His breeches were worn, with mending around the knees and the bottom of the material was frayed and torn.

Aethelhard walked to the window, placing his hands on the sill, looking over the garden. "Is there time for a walk before supper?"

"Yes, milord." The servant moved nervously from one foot to the other as he awaited Aethelhard's command.

Aethelhard picked up his cloak and walked toward the door. "I'll take a short walk in the garden. Send someone for me if I've not returned before supper."

Aethelhard walked out of the castle and immediately felt the warmth of the last rays of sun on his face. Soon the cool night air would surround the garden and the land with a blanket of mist. He walked through the garden reflecting on his plight. Here, the garden was dense, and the large overhanging trees made it feel more secluded. He stopped suddenly, as he heard something just a head of him. He pressed his body against the wall of roses and felt thorns prick his arms. Placing his hand where his sword should have been then cursing softly as he felt nothing. He left his weapons in his chambers. A stupid thing to do even in the safety of Hutton's high castle. Staying close to the wall of roses, he turned the bend and saw a young woman. Her back was to him as she sat curled on a bench, her head resting in her hands. Even from this far away, Aethelhard recognized the strawberry blonde hair. His body relaxing, he walked toward her.

"Good eve," he said.

Startled, she raised her head, her hands quickly moving over her cheeks. "Good eve. I didn't hear you coming. No one comes to this part of the garden."

Aethelhard looked carefully at her, and in the setting rays of the sun he caught a glint on her cheek. "I hope I didn't disturb you."

"No."

He nodded to the bench she was sitting on. "May I join you?"

Kylin brushed a small curl from her cheek. The curl was damp, and he noticed the sadness that enveloped her.

After a minute or two of awkward silence he said, "Lovely eve."

"Yes, it is," she replied softly.

Aethelhard glanced to her. "Is something wrong?"

Kylin looked away quickly. "No."

Aethelhard averted his eyes from her. "It looks as though you've been crying."

Kylin slowly turned toward him. "It doesn't concern you."

"Perhaps not," Aethelhard said.

She picked a rose from the bush that was beside her. Her fingers running over the soft petals stopping as she felt a drop of dew hidden deep within its velvet folds. "It seems even the roses know of my sadness."

Aethelhard sat next to her and rested his hands on the bench.

"It's father," she spoke softly.

"He mentioned he needed to speak with you." Aethelhard shifted on the bench and looked toward the dining hall.

Kylin nodded. "He spoke with me."

Aethelhard looked back to her. Her fingers were still moving over the petals of the rose, her eyes watching the petals bend, then return to their natural shape after her fingers left them.

His eyes moved away from her and toward the moon that was now visible and rising over the darkening horizon.

Kylin took a deep breath, her eyes never leaving the rose. "Father wishes me to marry Lord Claec Quintrell."

Aethelhard nodded. "He's an exceptionally good choice. Your lands are close and could be joined. He is also a courageous warrior from what I've been told."

"I don't love him," she said throwing the rose in front of her. It fell on the path in the soft rays of the rising moon.

Aethelhard turned to her. "You don't love him? When has that stopped a wedding? Love will come later."

Kylin looked at him as tears started to trickle down her cheeks. "I knew you wouldn't understand."

"What's there to understand?" Aethelhard spoke puzzled.

"You are too much like father."

"He's a wise man," Aethelhard said.

"He knows nothing of love," her voice rising.

"He loves you as a father should," Aethelhard said calmly

"But has he ever experienced love?" she said standing.

"You learn to love and respect the one you are bound to," Aethelhard said.

"I knew you would side with father." She turned running down the path.

Aethelhard watched as she vanished into the garden. He shook his head. Love was earned through devotion and respect. It wasn't something that came to you. He looked at the rose on the path noticing its soft petals becoming wrinkled and wilted. He picked up the rose and tossed it into the bush.

He shook his head once more and started down the path toward the dining hall. What was this 'love' she spoke of?

Aethelhard walked into the large dining hall. Hutton was drinking mead as he waited for the others to arrive.

"Good eve," Hutton greeted him noticing the cloak he was wearing.

Aethelhard took off his cloak placing it over a chair by the door. "Good eve."

Pouring himself a mug of mead he looked toward the door. "Good eve, Lady Laila."

Hutton turned, nodding to his wife. "Good eve, my dear."

"I was hoping you would be able to join us for dinner," Laila spoke to Aethelhard.

"I would like to thank you for allowing me to stay here," Aethelhard said.

"Of course," she said. "You're a friend of the family."

Servants started bringing out platters of venison, dried fruit, potatoes, and fresh bread. Hutton looked toward the door, his brows furrowing a moment. "Where's Kylin?"

"She'll be here shortly. I left her room a few moments ago after speaking to her," Laila said looking over the food the servants were setting on the table.

Hutton shook his head. "She's not still speaking of this 'love', is she?"

"She's a young woman. She's learned of a different love from the bards' songs in the villages she visited during her travels."

Hutton looked back from the door and sat down. "Marriages are not built on this thing called love. I have arranged a very proper suitor for her. She'll marry Lord Quintrell."

Satisfied with the table, Laila sat down and filled her mug with mead. "Maybe we're taking things too quickly. I know Kylin can be difficult, but she has a sense of knowing what's best."

Aethelhard started toward the table then turned his head after hearing soft footsteps entering the room. He bowed. "Good eve, Kylin."

Hutton looked toward the door, then back to his wife. She smiled at him in a knowing way.

"It's good you could join us," Hutton said helping himself to the venison.

Kylin walked to the table and Aethelhard pulled out her chair. "Yes father." Aethelhard pushed her chair toward the table, then sat across from her.

"I hope you understand the arrangement," Hutton spoke as he filled his plate.

"I understand but I still don't agree," Kylin said.

Aethelhard helped himself to the food. He started to eat and looked to Kylin's plate. She'd placed very little on her plate and was picking at the food that was there. He felt the tension in the air and took another gulp of mead. Hutton looked at his daughter still picking at her food.

"You act as if you're sick," Hutton said to Kylin as he took another large bite of venison. He looked toward Laila. "Do you know what's wrong with her?"

Laila voice was calm. "I thought we'd already spoken about this."

Hutton looked from Laila then back to Kylin. He suddenly slammed his mug of mead on the table. "I'll not have you behaving like this, Kylin. We've company and your behavior for the last few days has been abominable. You're my daughter and you'll act as a proper lady should."

Aethelhard looked up from his plate looking first to Hutton, then to Kylin. Her head was bowed her long hair hiding her face.

"Did you hear me?" Hutton's face etching with anger.

Kylin finally looked up; tears streaming down her cheeks. "Yes, I heard you. How could I not hear you? You wish for me to marry Lord Quintrell and I'll marry him. But you can never make me love him."

The servants stood at the door leading into the dining hall not sure if they should enter to refill the table. One of them moved toward the door and Kylin threw her plate just missing him. "Leave traitors. I'll not have you listen to another of my conversations." She turned toward her father. "I'll take leave to my chamber now."

Hutton's face was crimson with anger and humiliation at his daughter's behavior. Kylin left the room before he could gather his wits. Laila stood quietly. "I'll tend to her."

"You'll do no such thing. We have company," Hutton spoke sternly. He motioned Geary to him placing a key in his hand. "Make sure she doesn't leave her room. Bring the key back to me as soon as the door is locked," he whispered not wanting anyone else to hear him. Geary nodded and quickly left the room.

"You can't keep her in her room forever," Laila said.

"No, but I can keep her there until she marries and becomes his problem." Hutton looked toward the door, the anger still in his face, then slowly turned toward Aethelhard. "What were you thinking about in the garden?"

Aethelhard looked up to him quickly. "Thinking about?"

Hutton refilled his mead and started eating his supper as if nothing had happened. "Yes, I often go to the garden to think as well. There's nothing there to distract me."

Aethelhard thought quickly not wanting to mention he saw Kylin while in the garden. "I was trying to remember if there's anything else about the castle or land that I could remember," Aethelhard said.

"Did you remember anything?" Hutton reached for a sweet roll on the table.

"No." Aethelhard said. His thoughts returning to the talk he and Kylin had in the garden. Whatever this love was, it was enough to anger Hutton.

Geary walked quietly into the room and gave Hutton the key.

"Are you sure she was in her room?" Hutton said as he put the key in his pocket.

"I heard someone in the room, but I didn't open the door, milord," Geary said.

Hutton nodded. "Very well. Go back to the kitchen. I'll let you know if anything else is needed."

Geary bowed and quickly left the room.

Laila walked out of the room without saying a word. Hutton started to say something to her, then shook his head finishing his mead.

"Kylin mentioned something about traitors before she left," Aethelhard said.

"It's nothing. She's a young woman with misguided ideas."

A few minutes later Laila ran breathless into the room. "She's gone!"

"What?" Hutton stood quickly causing his chair to fall on the stone floor.

"I went to her chambers to check on her and she was gone," Laila said.

"But how?" Hutton said looking for Cadda. "The door was locked. How do you know she's gone? How did you see inside her chambers?"

"The door—it was ajar. When I went inside, her chamber was empty."

Hutton turned to the door yelling for his knight, "Cadda!"

There was a commotion and yelling on the grounds before Cadda rushed into the room and bowed. "Yes, milord?"

"My daughter. She's missing. Search everywhere until she's found. No one sleeps until she's safe in her chambers."

"Yes, milord," Cadda said. Rushing out the door yelling for the other knights to join him. "Kylin is missing. All the grounds and buildings must be checked for her. If she was taken captive, they couldn't have gotten far. Look in the stable, the keep, and the chapel. Do not leave any stone unturned." Cadda's voice was trailing as the men quickly started to look for her.

Laila sat down, her angry eyes on her husband. "You shouldn't have forced her. She'd come to terms with this in time. Now she's gone."

Hutton walked to the hearth turning quickly to face his wife. "Kylin must learn to respect me and soon her husband. She must learn she has responsibilities. She's not a child anymore."

"I'll search for her as well," Aethelhard said as the argument became heated.

Hutton glared at his wife, then turned back to the hearth. "Fine, the more looking for her, the better. If you find her, you're to bring her to me immediately."

Aethelhard nodded grabbing his cloak and joining the other men in the search. There was much activity on the grounds as the men searched for Kylin. Cadda was giving orders on where to search next as the men came to him.

Aethelhard frantically looked over the grounds. He tried to remember when they were children where she'd hide. He looked toward the garden and remembered their talk before dinner. She said not many go to that part of the garden. Even if the knights had checked the garden, it was possible they might have missed her. His footsteps quickly carried him into the garden as he followed the same path he had before supper. He stayed close to the edge of the path where the foliage was dense, and thorns protruded among the roses. In the dim light of the moon, he saw the bench she'd been sitting on earlier, but she wasn't there. He continued to walk down the path walking deeper into the dense garden. He stopped by a willow tree with thick branches that sank to the ground his eyes scanning the garden.

"Looking for someone?"

Aethelhard jumped and pulled his sword from the sheath. He tried to look through the willow branches that formed a green curtain before him. A shadow moved under the branches toward him. Small pale hands parted the branches and Kylin stepped out.

"Are you alone?" Aethelhard tried to look through the willow branches for anyone who might be with her.

"Yes," Kylin said as she walked to him. "What has father got the men doing so late in the eve?"

"They're looking for you. Your father and mother are very worried since they didn't find you in your chambers." Aethelhard placed his sword back in its sheath. "We must return to the keep."

"No," she said defiantly.

Aethelhard turned toward her. "What do you mean, no?"

"Let them worry for a while. It will do them good." Kylin sat on a large rock, her fingers moving lightly over the willow branches rippling in the gentle breeze.

"I can't do that. I promised your father I'd return you if I found you." Aethelhard looked to the grounds and the men, then back to her. His palms were already becoming sweaty.

Kylin smiled to him. "What they do not know, will not hurt them."

Aethelhard walked to her. "Kylin, we must go." He reached down and gently took her arm.

"Let me go or I will call the knights and tell them you brought me here."

Aethelhard let go of her arm in disbelief. "How could you do such a dishonorable thing? We've been friends since childhood."

"The veil of childhood has been lifted. We're no longer the children we once were." Kylin looked toward the path, then moved quickly under the protective branches of the willow. "Quick, follow me, the knights are coming."

"No," Aethelhard said. "I must let them know I found you."

Kylin looked back to him, her fingers were parting the low overhanging branches of the willow. "Then I'll tell them you forced me here."

Aethelhard looked toward the advancing men, then back to her. "How will I know you will not betray me under the willow tree."

Kylin smiled playfully. "I suppose you'll have to choose who you wish to trust— me or Cadda's men." She passed through the branches of the willow letting them fall to conceal her once more.

Aethelhard looked toward the knights. They were only feet away. Against his better judgement, he quickly slipped behind the willow's green curtain just as the men approached. He started to speak softly, "Why…"

"Shhh," Kylin whispered. "Do you want them to hear us?"

"Why are we searching here?" one knight asked.

"Cadda said to search everywhere," the other knight said as his thick-gloved hands parted the thorny bushes.

"No one comes to this part of the garden anymore."

"All the more reason to search it. She can be a tricky one."

Aethelhard shifted under the tree causing a branch under his foot to snap. Kylin looked to him. "Be quiet," she whispered.

The knight's head quickly looked toward the willow tree.

"Did you hear something?"

The other knight looked toward the tree then shook his head. "No. Continue down the path. I'll follow in a moment."

Kylin and Aethelhard watched as the knight came closer to the tree then stopped as the other knight called down the path.

"I think I've found something."

He looked toward the tree then ran down the path. "I'm coming."

Kylin gave a sigh of relief. "It seems we've outwitted them this time."

"I wouldn't be so sure," one of the knights said parting the willow's branches. "How interesting. The Lord's guest is with the Lord's daughter who is betrothed. This will make for an interesting tale."

Kylin lunged toward him. "It's not what you think."

The knight grabbed her arm harshly. "We'll see," he laughed. "Cadda! I've found her!"

Cadda brought Kylin into the dining hall with Aethelhard behind them. Two knights were on either side of him. "Milord, your daughter has been found."

"Excellent," Hutton said raising a brow as Aethelhard was escorted behind them. "Where was she?"

"In the garden under a willow tree with your guest," Cadda said, his lips curling as he looked to Aethelhard.

Hutton looked to the Kylin then to Aethelhard. "I'm surprised at you. I thought you would have more honor than to seduce my daughter who is betrothed."

"I…" Aethelhard started to speak.

"It was not his fault, father," Kylin spoke. "He found me first and wanted to bring me to you."

"Then why did he not do as honor would demand of him?" Hutton said.

Kylin looked down for a moment, then back to her father's eyes. "I wouldn't let him."

Hutton looked to Laila, then back to the two. "Is there a plot between you two?"

"No! If anyone is to blame for this, it's me. Aethelhard had nothing to do with it. He was going to do the honorable thing."

"Then he should've done the honorable thing and brought you here. Now he has placed questions in my mind of his intent in coming here." Hutton walked toward the two. "Perhaps he even had a hand in getting you out of your room this eve. He was eager to look for you."

"No," Kylin said.

"Then how did you escape?" Hutton turned his angry eyes to Kylin. "You couldn't have escaped without help. Geary, my most trusted servant, was the one who locked your chamber door. I trust him above all my other servants."

"He didn't lock the door," Kylin finally said quietly.

Hutton turned away from them. "Enough! I'll not have such treachery in my own castle. Cadda, take Kylin to her chambers for the eve and post a knight outside her door. If she escapes, I'll hold you personally responsible." Hutton turned and looked to Aethelhard. "This has also cast tarnish on our relationship. I'll reconsider our agreement this eve. If I decide that your action this eve was dishonorable, I'll ask you to leave at sunrise tomorrow." He turned toward Cadda. "Take Aethelhard to his chambers, take his sword, and post a knight outside as well. I have much to think about this eve." Hutton walked out of the dining hall with Laila following close behind.

Cadda turned toward the two. He nodded toward one of the knights. "You'll keep watch over Kylin." Turning toward Aethelhard, he smiled with contempt. "I'll watch over you this eve. If you try to escape, it'll be the last time you make that mistake," Cadda laughed.

Once in their chambers, Hutton ran his fingers through his hair and kicked the pail of wood beside the hearth in their room. Geary moved tentatively toward the spilled wood and started to pick it up.

"You did lock the door, did you not?" Hutton angrily turned toward him.

Geary dropped a piece of wood and quickly picked it up. "Yes, milord."

"Are you absolutely sure?"

"Yes, milord"

Hutton turned and grabbed the front of Geary's tunic until his feet were almost off the floor. "You wouldn't lie to me, would you?" Hutton's face was crimson as the anger filled him again.

Geary's eyes became large and he shook his head fiercely. "No, milord. I would never disobey your command."

Laila's hand gently touched Hutton's shoulder. "Let him go. He has done no harm this eve. Kylin was found safe."

Hutton released the man's tunic causing him to drop quickly to the floor. Geary stumbled then started to collect the rest of the wood. "She was with Aethelhard, if you remember," Hutton said.

"Yes, I remember. But he didn't harm her."

"At least my own men know what honor is and obey my command. I had a feeling he would be trouble." Hutton turned toward the hearth and brought the mug of mead to his lips.

"Why do you say that?"

He finished the mead, then refilled his mug. "He's a young man. There's much that he must learn. Honor for one it seems."

"Are you going to help him?" Laila asked as her servant started to remove her gowns.

"I don't know," Hutton said, his back to her.

"There was no harm done."

Hutton spun around. "Not this time but how can I trust his intentions after this eve? Why did he not bring Kylin to me as instructed?"

"You know she can be persuasive," Laila said.

Hutton took a deep breath and turned back to the hearth.

"Milord, would you like to prepare for bed?" Geary spoke softly.

Hutton nodded setting his mead down and held out his arms as his tunic was removed. Hearing a commotion in the courtyard, Hutton quickly walked to the door of his chambers as Cadda came running up the stairs.

"Milord, we must speak," Cadda said.

"Who's escaped?" Hutton said as he pushed Geary away and put on his tunic.

"Kylin and Aethelhard are secured in their chambers. I left my best knights to watch over them."

"Then what is it?" Hutton said curtly.

"The battles. They are not going well," Cadda said. "A messenger has returned from the battlefront. Most of your men are dead from the battle a few days ago. The enemy is advancing. They are using Aethelhard's castle as a stronghold."

Hutton turned away. "Is that all? There's no other news?"

"No," Cadda said.

"Resume your post."

"Yes, milord," Cadda bowed and left.

"What are you going to do?" Laila asked as her servant brushed her long hair.

"I don't know," Hutton said walking to the hearth. He finished his mead and had Geary refill his mug.

Laila sat up in the large bed. She pulled the blankets that had been warmed by the fire over her. "There must be something you can do."

Hutton continued to drink his mead in silence.

Laila watched him for a moment. "Hutton, did you hear me?"

"Yes," his voice was soft.

"How long will it be until they lay siege to our castle? They must be getting close." Laila's voice was urgent.

Hutton ran his fingers through his hair, then threw his mug into the hearth causing the fire to expand briefly as the alcohol burned. "What choice do I have?" He turned to look at her. "I'll have to help Aethelhard and hope that I can trust his word. They haven't advanced here so they must be using Elwyn as a place to strengthen their armies. The only way to stop them, is to take back Elwyn castle and put some distance between our castle and the Scots." He turned back to the hearth taking another deep breath. "I only hope he is enough like his father that he will be able to rule once he has command of the castle. In the meantime, we need to keep him away from Kylin. I want no more trouble."

"I'm sure that he'll be able to rule once he has his castle back." Laila was starting to settle under the warm blankets.

Hutton undressed and joined her. "He's still young."

"That could be good," Laila said.

"Youthfulness can be a strength and a detriment," Hutton said. "The body is strong, but knowledge is lacking. I'll test him tomorrow as we go over the plans for the siege."

Chapter 2

The light of dawn was just breaking when Aethelhard awoke with a rap at the door. "Yes?" He rubbed his eyes and sat up in the large bed.

"Milord D'arcy is ready to see you," the knight posted outside his chamber door replied.

"I'll be ready in a few minutes." Aethelhard placed his feet on the cold stone floor walking to the chair where his clothes lay. After dressing and putting on his cloak, he approached the knight posted outside his door. "Where's Hutton?" He looked to the knight as he placed his hand on his belt where his sword usually was. "Or am I to be escorted?"

The knight moved from the door. "Milord D'arcy is in the keep. He said to meet him at the door, and he would take you inside."

Aethelhard walked outside the building just as the sun was peeking over the edge of the horizon. The laundress was hanging laundry on the line, a young boy was throwing seed for the chickens, and the smell of fresh bread filled the air. He looked over the nearby village with their houses made of wattle and daub, the men plowing the fields and children running through the streets playing with sticks and a rounded melon. Everything was running the way it should. Movement caught his eye and he nodded to the two knights and marshal who were watching him. He saw Hutton standing in the doorway as he approached the keep. "Good morn," Aethelhard said.

Hutton handed Aethelhard his sword. "Yes, it does look as if it will be a good morn."

Aethelhard took his sword. "I assume you've made your decision."

Hutton nodded and motioned him toward the door. "You may stay."

"No conditions?" Aethelhard asked walking inside.

Hutton paused for a moment, then shook his head. "No conditions." Hutton led him down the hallway and into a small windowless room. There were candles mounted on the walls and some on the large table. "We need to plan the siege," Hutton said sitting down at the table. "I had breakfast brought here so we can start immediately."

Aethelhard sat down pouring a cup of mead. "Where would you like to start?"

"How many men do you believe Blackmon had for the siege?" Hutton said picking up a piece of bread.

"It's hard to say. It seemed like hundreds," Aethelhard said setting down his cup of mead.

"You must have seen the camp they set up nearby."

"They were in the forest. It was difficult to see exactly how many men or what weapons he had," Aethelhard said.

"Didn't you send spies in?" Hutton questioned.

"Of course, we did. They never came back although we heard screaming from the forest the eve after they left."

Hutton leaned back in his chair. "Did they volunteer?"

Aethelhard looked to him. "Yes, why do you ask?"

"How do you know the screams you heard were the screams of death? Could they have been screams of forgery?"

"No," Aethelhard said standing. "All of my father's men were loyal."

"How do you know? You said a traitor let Blackmon's army in. Maybe there were more."

Aethelhard clinched his fists, anger starting to once more rule his thoughts.

Hutton nodded to the parchment that was on the table. "Draw the castle and surrounding land. Mark any areas that you think could give us an advantage for the siege. We'll need a place to camp and ready our weapons. The trebuchets will help to weaken the castle walls while the minors dig under the castle wall to burn the timbers."

Aethelhard continued to sketch the castle and surrounding land. Finished, he pushed the parchment toward Hutton. "There's the castle and surrounding land. We'll have to be self-sufficient as the villagers are being ruled by terror. They won't risk their own death to help as long as Blackmon is in the castle."

Hutton looked over the parchment and nodded. "We'll have to watch for traitors as well. How long did it take you to get here?"

"About two days," Aethelhard said. "My journey was longer due to the circumstances at my castle. I had to journey by night and keep out of sight of everyone. The journey is usually one day by horseback."

Hutton leaned back in the chair. "Blackmon will be expecting the siege. There's no way we'll be able to hide the advancement of men and weaponry."

"We could camp in the forest as Blackmon did."

Hutton shook his head. "No, Blackmon probably has men in the forest. The same cover that would hide us would hide the enemy as well. They could fire down on us from the trees. We'll approach this siege with no hiding of weaponry or men."

Aethelhard looked at the parchment again then placed his finger to the edge of the village. "There's a place here, we could stay as we ready for the siege."

Hutton leaned over the table and looked at the parchment. "What's there?"

Aethelhard continued. "It is a grazing area for the village animals. There's a small hill leading down from the village and a flat valley below. We could post men on the hill to watch for Blackmon and his men."

"It will be difficult to move the heavy weaponry over the hill," Hutton said.

"There's a small hill. Here to the right, the land is flat. The hill would hide our advancement for a brief period. It's far enough away from the castle we could watch Blackmon but close enough for the trebuchets to reach the castle."

Hutton nodded. "That might work. What about the castle's defenses from this side?"

"There's a drawbridge with a guard tower that goes over the moat. Water from a stream runs over the rocks to the side of the guard tower and into the moat. This keeps the moat full."

"We can't take our heavy weaponry through the moat or up the rocky side. How do you think we will be able to get inside?" Hutton said.

"I know of a way into the castle from the small waterfall around the moat."

"Does Blackmon know of this?" Hutton looked to Aethelhard.

Aethelhard laughed. "My father didn't know of this. It was something I discovered as a child. It's my secret place. I hadn't thought about it for years until yesterday."

"Go on," Hutton said.

"I need to make it to the waterfall. From there, I know a way in next to the guard towers. All that needs to be done is to overpower the guard and lower the drawbridge."

"Are you sure you want to do this? It will be risky," Hutton said.

"Yes," Aethelhard said firmly. "It's my castle. I'll be the first to enter or the first to die trying."

Hutton nodded. "It'll not be easy but it's the best chance we have." He pushed back his chair and taking the drawing, threw it into the hearth. The flames licked over the dry paper and soon all that remained were ashes. "I'll get the men assembled and the weaponry ready."

Aethelhard walked out of the room with Hutton. "Is there anything you need my help with?"

Hutton shook his head as he walked outside onto the grounds. "Cadda!"

There was a clamoring on the grounds as the knights called to each other. In a few minutes, Cadda came out of the defensive tower and bowed. "Milord, you wished to see me?"

"Yes. I need for you to assemble the knights and get them ready for a siege. Also, check over the weaponry and make sure everything is ready," Hutton said as he walked toward the chapel.

"Are you expecting a siege at the castle, milord?" Cadda questioned.

"No. We'll be travelling for the siege. Make sure everyone is ready. We'll be leaving within the week." Hutton walked into the chapel.

"Yes, milord. I'll have everything prepared."

There was much activity as the knights readied for the siege. Swords needed sharpened, equipment checked, and prayers said at the chapel.

Hutton turned to Aethelhard. "You may want to join me. We will need all the help we can get."

It was late in the evening when Aethelhard and Hutton finished praying at the chapel. The sun had set, and a cool wind was blowing over the grounds. The moon peeked through the cloudy sky now and then as they walked to the main hall.

"It smells like rain," Hutton said.

Aethelhard looked at the sky and nodded. "The wind does signal a change."

"The rain will make it difficult to get to the castle," Hutton said as he opened the door.

"Depends on how much rain falls."

The servants brought out a thick stew filled with venison and vegetables. Fresh baked bread, butter, and a plate of cheese were brought out as well.

"Will Kylin and Laila be joining us for supper?" Aethelhard asked sitting down.

Hutton looked toward him. "No, I'm sure they already had supper and are preparing for bed." Hutton looked to Geary as he spoke, and the servant nodded his head in agreement.

After finishing supper, Hutton started toward his chambers. "I think I'll prepare for bed as well. The chilly wind is making a warm bed seem even more inviting."

Aethelhard walked outside and looked to the dark sky seeing more clouds forming. "It looks as if it will rain," he said walking back inside."

Once inside his chamber, Aethelhard warmed himself by the hearth. Even though it was late, he could not sleep. Thoughts of the siege kept running through his mind. Finally, he picked up his cloak and walked back into the biting wind. Maybe a walk would clear his mind.

He nodded to a knight walking past him. The wind swirled around him as he walked toward the forest. Maybe the trees would shield him from the wind so he could continue his walk. He stopped as he approached the forest and saw shadows moving through the trees. His hand moved to the hilt of his sword, his body tensing after hearing voices. He crouched behind a bush and tried to listen.

The two men stopped and looked around quickly making sure there was no one around. Through the darkness, Aethelhard saw one wore a cloak and the other a helmet of some kind.

The figure wearing the helmet handed something to the one who wore a cloak. "Take this and make sure it makes it to its destination. You must travel as quickly as you can. You must deliver it directly to him in person and no one else." The other figure nodded.

Aethelhard strained through the whistling wind, cursing under his breath as a branch snapped beneath his foot. The men stopped their conversation and looked in the general direction the sound came from. They quickly finished their conversation and parted ways.

Aethelhard remained motionless until he was sure they were gone. His brows furrowed as he walked toward the castle. He recognized one of the voices but could not remember who it belonged to.

"Are you still awake?" Laila stirred from her sleep to find Hutton standing by the hearth.

Hutton turned away from the hearth. "Yes."

"What's keeping you awake?"

He walked to the window, pulling back the heavy tapestry that hung over it. "It's nothing. I'll be to bed soon." He looked absently over the land then stopped as he saw a cloaked figure walking from the forest toward the castle. He pulled the cloth open a little more to see better. He recognized the figure as Aethelhard. His fingers drummed over the stone wall as he watched him walk slowly to the castle. Now and then Aethelhard would look behind him as if he expected to see someone. Hutton's eyes narrowed for a moment and his fingers slipped from the cloth.

He opened the door of his chambers and yelled down the hall, "Cadda!" Cadda came running down the hall stopping at the door of his chambers.

"Yes, milord?" he said.

"My daughter. Have you seen her?"

"She was safe in her chambers only an hour ago," Cadda replied.

"Are you sure? Have you checked on her?" Hutton said anger filling his voice.

"I have not personally checked on her, milord. I did post a knight at her door as instructed." Cadda's face was puzzled.

"Check on her. Make sure she is still in her chamber. I want to know if she is or is not in her chamber."

Cadda saw Hutton's hands were clenched at his side. "Yes, milord. I will personally check on her and report back to you in a few minutes."

Hutton left the door ajar and walked to the window once more pulling the tapestry away. His fingers drummed over the cold stones as he thought.

Laila stirred and sat up. "What is wrong?"

"There is

nothing wrong. Why do you ask?" Hutton turned away from the window.

"I heard you talking with Cadda. Why did you want him to check on Kylin? There is a guard posted outside her door."

Hutton started to pace the floor. "I just saw Aethelhard come back from the forest."

Laila yawned. "He must have been unable to sleep just as you. Perhaps he took a walk."

Hutton stopped and turned to her. "He told me he was going to his chamber to prepare for bed. When he walked out of the forest, he kept looking behind him as if he was expecting someone. Why did he leave his chamber and not tell me? Who did he meet in the forest?" Hutton turned hearing a soft knock on the door. "Yes?"

Cadda stepped into the room. "I personally went into her room and checked on her. Kylin is sleeping peacefully."

Hutton turned back to the hearth. "You may leave."

Cadda bowed and left the chamber. "Yes, milord."

Laila was awake now and looked to her husband. "Why should it bother you Aethelhard took a walk? It's not like you to be suspicious of him."

Hutton quickly turned toward her. "He was with our betrothed daughter, alone, under a willow tree in the dark. What else should I think?"

"Not tonight. Tonight, he was only taking a walk. Yet you falsely accuse him of trying to seduce Kylin. She's already admitted it was her doing that Aethelhard didn't bring her back right away."

"But by honor, he should have," Hutton spoke with anger.

"That's no reason to accuse him of similar acts tonight. Cadda has already looked in on Kylin. She's asleep in her chamber," Laila said, her own frustration building.

Hutton walked back to the window and moved the tapestry. "It doesn't matter. Kylin's betrothed, Lord Quintrell, will be here tomorrow morning. We'll see what happens after his arrival."

Hutton returned to bed although he slept a fitful night. Why was Aethelhard walking and looking back behind him in the forest? Was there someone else in the forest as well? Why did he not return Kylin when he found her under the willow? These questions and many more kept running through his head until the morning came with the hope of a quick wedding. Then he would know if Aethelhard was true to his word. He opened the door a crack hearing quick footsteps toward Kylin's chamber. It was only Maria. Now that Kylin was with her servant, he had no reason to worry about her.

"Milady Kylin wake up. Today's an important day." Maria said as she tried to wake her.

Kylin pulled the covers over her head to quiet Maria. "Why is today different from yesterday?"

"Milord Quintrell is coming to the castle this morn. You must get up so I can dress you. It is a special day. Milady must look her best for her future husband."

Kylin threw back the blankets and sat up. "What?" Her feet quickly fell to the stone floor. "Who told you this?"

Maria busied herself preparing Kylin's bath. "Your father informed me of his arrival late last eve."

Kylin threw her pillow on the floor. "I will not see him!"

"But milady, he's your betrothed."

"He is not my betrothed. He's my father's betrothed. I didn't agree to this." Maria placed the fragrant oil with herbs in her bath. "Yes, milady." She stirred the water to mix the oil and to test the temperature. "The water is warm. You should bathe before it cools." She helped Kylin take off her bedclothes.

Kylin stood tense, as she was undressed then stepped into the warm water. Her eyes closed as the water surrounded her. She'd almost drifted to sleep when Maria woke her once more to bathe and dry her.

Maria had just finished dressing Kylin when the trumpets sounded announcing Lord Quintrell's arrival.

"We must hurry, milady. Milord Quintrell will be here shortly," Maria said as she placed the finishing touches on Kylin's dress and hair.

Kylin closed her eyes in defeat and nodded. "I'll be down in a few minutes." She sighed and looked out the small window hearing the swords clash as the men moved in rhythm.

"You'll have to do better than that, milord," the knight said with a smile.

Aethelhard laughed moving quickly toward him and their swords clashed again.

"Watch them closely. They are demonstrating footwork that is valuable if you are going to be a squire and win a match," said another knight.

"Except they are laughing," Kylin said walking toward them.

Aethelhard turned as she spoke, and the other knight put the tip of his sword to his throat.

"You should not let a lady distract you. Even a beautiful lady," the knight said.

Aethelhard moved slowly and with a quick move of his sword, the knight's sword was on the ground. "And you must never underestimate your competitor," Aethelhard said with a smile.

The knight bowed. "Your skills have bested me this time but there is always time for another match."

Aethelhard pushed the knight's sword toward him with his own sword. "I agree. Best two out of three?" Aethelhard turned his head hearing horses clopping over the drawbridge.

"Lord Quintrell approaches," the knight called from the guard tower.

Aethelhard put his sword back into his sheath. "We'll have to continue our lessons later."

Kylin looked toward the gate and fell silent as she watched her betrothed enter the grounds.

Hutton walked out of a nearby building, the steward still with a handful of papers and talking to him. "Enough!" Hutton finally said. "My daughter's betrothed is here. The papers will have to wait."

"But, milord," the steward stumbled.

Hutton turned toward him. "I said enough." He walked toward the man as he dismounted his horse. "Welcome to Nottes Castle, Claec."

"It is a pleasure to arrive," Claec said walking toward Hutton. Claec looked toward the group who only moments ago had been watching a training demonstration. He bowed and took Kylin's hand and kissed it. "You look lovely today, my dear."

Aethelhard noticed Kylin cringe as he kissed her hand. "Thank you, milord," she spoke after some hesitation. Now that Claec was closer Aethelhard looked over him finding something familiar about him. His brows furrowed.

"Claec, this is Lord Aethelhard Elwyn. He's also staying with us for a while. Aethelhard, this is Lord Claec Quintrell, Kylin's betrothed." Hutton emphasized "Kylin's betrothed." There was no doubt he wanted to make sure Aethelhard understood.

Aethelhard nodded. "It's a pleasure to meet you." Still, he couldn't stop looking at him as he tried to place where he'd seen him before.

One of the knights traveling with Claec brought a wooden container to him. "Your mead, milord."

Claec looked to the small wooden cask and not seeing any stains, smiled. "All of the casks made the trip, I see."

"Yes, milord," said the knight.

"They're all accounted for as well?" Claec asked.

"Yes, milord."

Claec took the small cask of mead and handed it to Hutton. "I think you'll enjoy the mead. It's a little something that I brought from my travels. Come, let us enjoy some."

Hutton smiled, looking at the casks of mead. "It is a time of celebration." He handed the cask to Geary. "Take this to the butler for the buttery. Let him know we will be at the main hall soon to enjoy some of the mead Claec so generously brought with him. Also, let Lady D'arcy know Lord Quintrell is here. She is to meet us in the main hall as well."

Geary bowed taking the cask of mead. "Yes, milord."

"Let us go to the main hall," said Hutton.

Claec offered his arm to Kylin. She looked to her father, then slowly took Claec's arm. Claec gently patted her hand and smiled. "I will have to get used to having a beautiful lady at my arm. Although I do not think it will take long." He smiled to Kylin and even from behind him, Aethelhard could see her cringe.

"Yes, milord," she spoke softly.

"Please, Kylin. It is Claec. No need for such formalities now that we are betrothed."

Kylin nodded walking toward the main hall.

Laila soon joined them. "Good eve, Claec," she said walking into the room.

Claec bowed. "Milady D'arcy, it is a pleasure to see you again. It is easy to see where Kylin gets her beauty."

Laila smiled. "Thank you."

The butler brought out the small cask of mead and opened it. He poured the mead into the goblets and left the room. Geary picked up two of the goblets and handed one to Hutton and one to Laila. He then handed a goblet each to Kylin and Claec with the last goblet to Aethelhard. Claec looked to Geary for a moment. The servant nodded indicating he had successfully put the nightshade in Kylin and Aethelhard's goblets.

Hutton put his goblet in the air as a toast. "To Claec and Kylin, may they always love as they do today."

They all drank of the mead.

"It's very good mead," Hutton mused finishing it.

"I am glad you like it," Claec said.

Hutton poured himself another goblet. "There is a lot we will need to go over for the wedding."

Claec looked to Kylin and smiled. "Yes, and the sooner we are wed, the better. I am not one to wait long for a treasure as Kylin."

"Good," Hutton said. "Circumstance dictate that the sooner the wedding happens, the better."

"Any reason why?" Claec poured another goblet of mead.

"I must leave soon on business."

"Will you require my assistance?" Claec asked.

"No, Aethelhard will go with me," Hutton nodded to Aethelhard.

Claec looked to Aethelhard, then back to Hutton as he took another drink of the mead. "I hope it is nothing that will put you in peril. I've heard of the many battles to the north of your land."

Hutton hesitated, then moved closer to Claec as he spoke quietly. "It is a siege to get Elwyn castle back."

Claec looked to Hutton curiously but with a smile. "Why so quiet about the plans?"

"The walls have ears," Hutton said. "It is difficult to say where the enemy lays in wait."

Claec nodded. "You are wise to keep such news as quiet as possible."

Kylin's head dropped for a moment, then jerked up as she opened her eyes quickly.

"I hope you're not getting bored with me already," Claec chuckled watching her closely.

Hutton looked to Kylin. "She's been looking forward all day for your visit. It's most likely the excitement that has made her tired."

Kylin placed her hand over her mouth as she yawned. "I'm suddenly tired, father. May I be excused to my chamber for the eve."

Hutton looked to her sternly for a moment then waved his hand. "Of course."

Claec stood and helped her from her chair. "I hope you feel well rested in the morning."

Kylin yawned as she stood. "I'm sure all I need is rest."

"Geary," Hutton called.

"Yes, milord."

Hutton motioned him closer and whispered so the others could not hear. "Speak to Cadda and have him post a guard outside her chamber door."

Geary nodded and left.

"I hope nothing is wrong," said Claec after seeing Hutton speaking quietly to Geary.

"It is nothing," Hutton said. He looked to Aethelhard and noticed him yawn as well.

"It seems that I am tired tonight as well," Aethelhard said as he stifled another yawn.

Claec chuckled. "It seems as if my very presence is putting your family and friends to sleep."

Hutton looked to Aethelhard and his eyes narrowed for a moment.

"No, I was assisting with the training of the young knights and squires this afternoon before you arrived," Aethelhard said.

Claec took another drink of the mead. "I wouldn't think a little sword training would wear out someone with your skills."

Aethelhard yawned again. "Nor I."

"Perhaps we should all retire for the night," Laila said.

Hutton looked to Aethelhard, then nodded. "There's much we need to plan tomorrow. It will do us good to get an early start on the day."

Hutton made sure there was a guard for Kylin's chamber door then followed Laila into their chamber.

"Didn't you find it rather odd that Kylin and Aethelhard were both tired this early in the eve," Laila said as she was changed into her night wear.

"Yes, I do," Hutton said. "That's why there's a guard at her chamber door. There will not be any walks tonight." He leaned over and blew out the candle.

Chapter 3

Aethelhard awoke late during the night with his head pounding. He opened his bleary eyes and tried to stand but stumbled. He grabbed onto a vine only to hit his head on a tree. Once more, the blackness closed around him.

The next time he awoke he was disoriented in the forest. He sat groggy and rubbed his head still trying to remember how he got here. All he could remember was feeling tired and retiring to his chamber last eve. His fingers moved over his head, stopping at the knot and he cringed in pain. His hand on a tree, he started to pull himself up pausing now and then to keep his balance. Finally standing, he took an unsteady step, his hand once more grabbing hold of the tree.

He leaned against the tree and saw that it was light. He must have spent all night in the forest. He looked over his torn clothes and once again wondered what happened last night.

He looked ahead and saw knights running over the castle grounds. It looked as if they were searching for someone or something. Kylin must have escaped during the night. Unsteadily, he started to walk toward the clearing just outside the trees, his hand occasionally reaching for a tree to unsteady him.

A knight roughly grabbed him and called out. "I found him."

Through the blur around him, he saw men running toward him. Hutton and Claec pushed through the knights.

"Where is she?" Hutton said as he pushed on Aethelhard. He fell to the ground, his mind still spinning.

"Who?" Aethelhard said weakly as he tried to stand. The knight who found him roughly pulled him to his feet. Claec threw a punch, which hit him square in the jaw, and he fell back to the ground. The knights pulled him back to his feet.

"Where is she? What did you do with Kylin?" Claec was close enough to him, he could smell his sour breath of last night's mead.

"I don't know," Aethelhard responded. "I am not even sure how I got into the forest."

"Liar!" Claec shouted and started to throw another punch. Hutton grabbed hold of his arm.

"Enough!" Hutton said. "He'll be of little use to us if you kill him."

Claec looked over his clothes. "She must have put up a good fight. Look how torn his clothes are and the knot on his head."

Aethelhard looked to the two men, his head still spinning. "I didn't take her. I have no idea where she is or what happened to her."

Claec started to charge toward him only to be stopped by two knights. "Liar!" He shouted again.

Hutton glared at Aethelhard then looked to the knights on either side of him. "Take him to the underground cell. Once I decide what to do, I'll send for him."

"Yes milord," the knight said. They grabbed hold on either side of him. If it were not for the fact, they had a tight hold on him, Aethelhard would have welcomed the help. The blackness threatened to surround him once more as he stumbled desperately trying to stay on his feet. He saw the others staring at him as he was led to the cell. When they passed Laila, she turned away.

They started down the stairs and Aethelhard stumbled. One of the knights cursed. "I guess we'll have to carry him down the stairs."

Through the fog in his head, Aethelhard weakly said, "I can make it."

The knight chuckled. "Not bloody likely. You could barely walk on level ground." They reached down and picked him up by his shoulders and Aethelhard cringed. He had not noticed his shoulders hurting as much as his head until now. Finally, at the bottom of the stairs, they finished carrying him to his cell. The door creaked opened and they pushed him inside the dark cell. Aethelhard stumbled, his hands against the damp earthen walls as he heard the door slam shut. He turned with his back against the wall.

"Take this key and make sure he doesn't escape. No one is to see him except by personal order of Milord D'arcy," he heard one of the knights telling the one who guarded the cells.

The guard chuckled, "I doubt he would make it very far even if he did escape."

As his back moved down the wall and he sat on the cold dirt, he heard the knights walking up the stairs. The others were talking quietly in the darkness but with the fog surrounding him, he couldn't make out their words. Slowly his mind drifted between sleep and the voices, sleep finally winning.

He was awakened with a loud banging on the bars. "Wake up, you fool." He opened his eyes and noticed the pounding in his head that had plagued him most of the day was finally gone. Slowly he stood up. "Here." Cadda pushed through a piece of bread and a cup of ale. "Be thankful Lord D'arcy is compassionate. I wouldn't have given you this."

"Then keep your bread and ale. Give it to the hounds. I have no need for anyone's compassion," Aethelhard said.

Cadda cursed and dropped the bread and ale outside the bars. "You're still rather arrogant for one who is in a locked cell. It means nothing to me if you eat or not. Milord only said to bring this down to you. I have obeyed his order." Cadda walked down the tunnel that led to the stairs, stopping to yell at one of the guards. Aethelhard heard the thud of his boots as he walked up the stairs.

Aethelhard sat down and rubbed the knot on his head. The fog had lifted from his head but that only made the knot hurt more. He tried to think through what happened during the last day and why they would suspect him of taking Kylin. Once more he saw Claec's face and tried to remember where he had seen him. The sound of horses walking by the small slit of a window at the top of the earthen cell suddenly jogged his mind. Claec had been the man bidding against him at the market for his steed. But it didn't make sense. He couldn't imagine a Lord of his standing bidding on a horse. He'd have someone else do it for him. And that still didn't explain what happened to Kylin.

He stood and walked toward the bread and ale Cadda dropped by the cell door. Maybe if he had a little something to eat and drink it would make more sense. He took a bite of the bread then brought the ale to his lips stopping suddenly. There was a different, yet familiar smell to the ale. He moved the ale from his lips and smelled the contents. His mind racing back to the previous night, he remembered the mead he was served had the same smell to it. He had thought nothing of it since it was a mead Claec bought from another land, but this was too much of a coincidence. He dipped his finger into the ale and tasted it. It had the same sweet taste of the mead. Someone must have put a sleep potion into his mead last night. Who ever it was, wanted him asleep again. He looked down the tunnel and not seeing anyone poured the ale into the chamber pot that was in his cell. If someone wanted him to sleep, he was not going to disappoint him. Aethelhard ate the rest of the bread and set the empty cup outside his cell. He then sat down and closed his eyes.

Soon he heard the stairs creaking as someone walked down them. The footsteps came closer to his cell.

"It looks as if he was hungry after all."

"But is the ale gone?"

Aethelhard recognized the first voice as Cadda's and the second as Claec's.

"Should be. Put him asleep for almost a day last time he was given the potion," chuckled Cadda.

Claec looked down the tunnel and at the other cell. "Are you sure no one else is here."

"Of course, milord," said Cadda.

"What about the walls and the small slit above the cell?"

Cadda laughed. "The only sound these walls have heard is moaning and screaming. I instructed my men to watch the slit in case Aethelhard tried to dig his way out. They would have called if they saw anything suspicious."

"Could he dig his way out? He can't escape."

"Do not worry. No one has ever escaped these cells," Cadda said confidently.

A sound of coins was heard and Aethelhard opened his eyes a little to see Claec place the bag of gold within Cadda's hand.

"Are they all there?"

"Count them if you wish," said Claec.

Cadda started to open the bag when they heard footsteps on the stairs. Cadda quickly hid the bag in his coat.

"Go down toward the second cell. Stay close to the wall. You can not be seen there," instructed Cadda.

Aethelhard also heard footsteps and then another voice.

"I must hurry. Milord will miss me if I am gone too long."

Aethelhard opened his eyes a slit to see Geary following behind Cadda.

"It's Geary," said Cadda as he approached the second cell.

Claec moved away from the wall and Aethelhard heard another bag of coins drop.

"You have done well mixing the potions," Claec said. "I might have use for you at my castle."

"No, milord," Geary said nervously. "It would raise the Lord's suspicions if I left suddenly."

Claec smiled. "It does not matter. You'll work at my castle soon enough."

"Maybe we could say you were poisoned," chuckled Cadda.

"Milord would never believe that. He knows my skills in mixing potions as I have taken care of his family for many years." Geary looked nervously over the area, then spoke softly. "Has Kylin awaken yet?"

Claec quickly slapped the servant. "I told you never to mention her name here," Claec said through gritted teeth.

Geary cowered down placing his hands over his head, dropping his bag of coins. "I'm sorry, milord. I only wanted to know if she had awakened yet. I gave her more potion than I should have." Geary looked to Cadda who was now glaring at him.

"Get out!" Claec said to Geary. "And remember what will happen if you ever breath a word of this to anyone—or mention her name again."

Geary quickly picked up his bag of coins, his voice heard as he ran down the tunnel. "Yes, milord."

Claec turned toward Cadda. "Make sure he leaves."

Cadda walked down the tunnel, as Geary's footsteps grew softer on the stairs. He watched as the knight shut the door to the dungeon then walked back to Claec. "He's gone, milord."

Claec started to pace the tunnel by the second cell. "What will become of him?"

"Aethelhard?" questioned Cadda.

"Yes. We cannot take a chance of him getting back to his castle or finding her," Claec said tensely.

Cadda shrugged. "Depends on what Milord D'arcy decides in the morning. He has retired to his chamber for the night. Nothing will be done until at least morning."

Aethelhard shifted and moaned softly. Both men turned quickly toward him.

"He's awake?" asked Claec.

Cadda laughed. He lifted the cup and turned it upside down. "The cup is empty. He'll sleep for quite some time. I instructed Geary to put more of the potion in his ale than the mead he had last evening. If he dies," Cadda shrugged, "it's one less problem we have to worry about."

Claec looked toward Aethelhard then motioned toward the tunnel. "We must get back."

As soon as Aethelhard was certain the two men left, he stood and lightly shook the bars. The door was securely locked. He knew he had to find a way out of the dungeon to find Kylin and clear his name. He looked frantically at the small slit that was designed to bring in fresh air but realized it was too narrow to dig out.

He sat down running his fingers through his hair. Even if he did find a way out, how was he going to find Kylin? He had no idea of where they had taken her. Unless— they had taken her somewhere in the forest. That must be where she is. But he still had to find a way out of this cell.

He looked toward the bars as he heard a clink. He had not heard anyone coming down the stairs. Cautiously, he walked toward the bars. His eye catching the glint of something on the hard ground. He crouched down and picked up a key. A vision of Laila came to him. He shook his head to clear his mind then looked around again. He tried the key in the rusted lock. The lock clicked and he pushed the bars open. With his back against the wall, he moved slowly through the tunnel in case the key was part of a trap. He started to climb the stairs then remembered the creaking. Slowly, he placed his foot on the outside of each step. There was no creaking of the wood. He continued up the stairs slowly, his heart pounding. Finally reaching the top. He pressed against the wall to see where the guard was posted. To his surprise, the guard was gone and the room empty. He paused by the door. He looked cautiously over the room not seeing anyone but still…he could see the faint vision of Laila. Moving quietly, he opened the door slowly and disappeared into the darkness.

Aethelhard reached the forest and melted into the shadows. He looked through the thick foliage sinking deeper into the curtain of darkness that was only interrupted by thin rays of the setting sun piercing the gloom of the falling night. His head turned as he heard someone coming toward the forest. He crouched by a thick shrub and listened to the men.

"Where do you think he went?" the first man said.

Aethelhard peered through the leafy branches and saw they were knights from the castle.

"He could be in the forest," the second knight said.

Aethelhard moved back just as one of the knight's swords cut through the shrub. He stayed motionless behind the thinner wall of leaves. One of the knights sat down on a rotting log.

"It's going to be difficult to search the forest at night. You never know what may be lurking here."

The second knight sat down on a rock next to the log. "But if we find him, we split the 50 gold pieces."

"How did he escape? "

"No one knows. The cell door was open when the guard went down to check on him. The guard claimed he never left his post at the top of the stairs. No one had been to the dungeon since Cadda checked on him."

The knight shifted on the log. "What happened to Lord Quintrell?"

"Aethelhard must have taken him prisoner in case he was caught. Lord Quintrell could be used as protection."

"Cadda said Lord Quintrell could be injured."

The knight moved on the rock then stood. "Lord Quintrell's room was a mess. A table was broken and the curtains from his bed were torn down." The knight walked away from the rock and looked through the darkening forest. "There was a trail of blood leading from his room to the outside."

"No one heard anything?" The knight moved from the log.

"There was not a knight near his chamber when it happened. Lord Quintrell could be dead by now."

The knights' voices drifted to silence as they walked away but Aethelhard had heard all that he needed. He knew he must find Kylin and Lord Quintrell. He had to restore his honor. But who would kidnap both and why?

Aethelhard slowly moved from the shrub, his eyes looking cautiously over the forest. He started to walk deeper into the forest knowing he would be at anyone's mercy that surprised him. His sword had been removed before he was taken to the dungeon. He would have to rely on his cunning and wits if he were found. There would be no bargaining for his release.

He stopped by a stream and reached down to take a drink as he tried to think of a plan. He remembered the men he heard talking the night before. It would be risky trying to get back to that spot since it was so close to the edge of the forest. If he could get there uncaught, he could wait to see if anyone would come back.

After walking a while, Aethelhard saw the clearing ahead. He looked over the area to see if anything was familiar and crept slowly to the spot where he'd heard the men talking. With luck, someone would come by.

There was not a sound of another human in the forest. Aethelhard thought the hunt for him must have stopped until daybreak. He waited with the sounds of the forest surrounding him. He listened as an owl called from a tree not far from him.

Several hours passed and his eyes grew heavy. The sounds of the forest had long stopped and all he heard was his own breathing. Aethelhard started to drift to sleep when a man's voice startled him awake. He crouched behind a fallen tree, listening, waiting as the footsteps came closer.

The man was cursing softly, rubbing his head. Aethelhard peered through the leaves of a fallen tree and finally saw him. It was Geary and he was coming closer with each footstep. Aethelhard watched as Geary walked past the tree.

"Bloody, tree," he mumbled. Geary stopped and looked over the forest. He had a heavy pack on his back but looked unarmed. Still, Aethelhard could not take any chances. There could be others close by but maybe Geary would lead him to Kylin. Geary adjusted the large pack and started through the woods once more. Aethelhard followed behind him using the thick brush to stay well hidden.

Geary continued through the forest looking back now and then to make sure he wasn't being followed. He stopped at the stream where Aethelhard had stopped at earlier. Geary followed the stream, careful to only step on the rocks that were beside it so as not to leave footprints in the soft mud. Aethelhard looked for an alternate route to follow Geary. If he took the rocks along the path, he would certainly be spotted but he couldn't let him get out of sight.

Aethelhard followed him through the tangled trees and vines. It was difficult for him to stay very close as he quietly fought his way through the undergrowth. He almost lost him twice but continued following the stream and eventually caught up with him.

Geary stopped suddenly and turned to look behind him. Aethelhard stopped staying as close as he could without being seen. Satisfied he was not being followed; Geary stepped from the rocks by the stream and started to wind through the forest. Aethelhard found it harder to follow him yet keep enough distance between them that he would not be spotted. The brush became thicker and Aethelhard was sure he'd lost him. He saw Geary disappear into a thicket of briers. He crouched down in the brush and waited. After a few minutes, he heard stirring and looked through the leaves of the tree to see Geary walk through a small hole in the briars.

He waited until he was sure Geary couldn't spot him, then moved closer to the briers hoping the cover of darkness would keep him hidden. As he approached the briers and looked through them, he saw a little clearing and then the mouth of a cave. He saw something move in the shadows of the cave.

"I thought he'd never get here," said one man

"I was getting hungry as well," said a second man.

"What kept him?"

"Something about the knights looking for someone. He had to wait until Lord D'arcy called off the hunt."

"Is that why Donnan or rather Milord Faulkner is here tonight?"

The other man nodded and continued to eat.

"Seems to be a lot of trouble just for a wedding," the man laughed.

"I don't think there will be a wedding."

"Why?"

The other man shrugged and took a drink of his ale. "Shame Geary couldn't get some of the mead Lord Faulkner brought. This ale is awful."

The men settled back against the cave entrance after eating their supper.

Chapter 4

Laila suddenly awoke. She blinked her eyes then saw an image of her Dalila. Her sister must be trying to reach her. That could only mean Kylin was in trouble. Laila closed her eyes purposely and saw Dalia's image as she told her where Kylin could be found. She glanced to Hutton making sure he was still asleep. Slowly, she slipped out of bed and put on an old dress. She dug under the bed until her fingers touched the rough edges of a shawl. She donned it carefully pulling it over her head and shoulders. She quietly closed the door to the keep and looked around for a cart or something. She found an old cart with straw in it and an old horse harnessed to it. That will work fine, she thought. It took the last of her strength hoping she could change her face. She checked it in the reflection of the trough of water. Satisfied, she climbed on the cart giving the reins a small shake. The horse trotted toward the draw bridge then she looked toward a guard. Seeing it was the old woman, he commanded the draw bridge open. The old woman nodded, and the cart moved over the dirt roads.

Aethelhard crept slowly toward the opening of the briars but after seeing there were more than two men and the weapons they had, he decided to wait. He moved back toward the briars and started to follow them around the cave. The briars gave way to more of the same thick brush that he'd been fighting most of the night.

He stopped noticing a gentle rise in the ground. That must be where the top of the cave is, he thought. He started to climb up the incline, but his foot slipped and poked into a hole that must be part of the cave wall. He stopped dead still and waited to see if anyone inside had noticed.

He looked toward the sky now that he was above the trees. A soft glow of light was starting in the east. It would soon be light. If he was going to find out if Kylin was in the cave, he had to do it now. The knights from the castle would soon be blanketing the forest to find him and collect their fifty gold pieces.

Lying flat on the curve of the ground, he placed his hand in the small hole his foot had originally made. The soft ground gave way and he started to pull the earth away slowly exposing a hole halfway down the cave's wall. It would be a snug fit, but it was the only way into the cave.

He moved until he was under the hole and slowly peered inside. Not seeing anyone, he hoisted him self toward the hole, wiggling his upper body so that his shoulders finally slipped between the rocks. He looked over the portion of the cave he could see. He was in a rather precarious position. If he were found, he would most certainly die.

He finally pulled himself through the hole and slid down the side until he was sitting on the damp dirt floor. His back was against the wall of the cave and he waited. His eyes were already adjusted to the darkness from the outside but inside the cave it seemed the inky darkness surrounded him like a glove.

After several minutes, he saw the dark contours of the cave and what looked to be a light coming from the direction of what he suspected was the front of the cave. With his back pressed against the wall, he followed the contours of the cave, staying close as possible to the shadows and darkness as he could. The light was getting stronger when he started to round a sharp contour of the cave wall. He stopped just as the contour started to bend back toward the cave wall. He closed his eyes for a moment listening for any sounds. He heard the scuff of boots nearby and knew it must be one of the guards. Slowly, he moved his head around the curve, keeping his body next to the contour of the stone cave wall.

He saw the guard sitting against the cave wall facing the other side of the wall. The guard's head was bobbing as he tried to stay awake. Aethelhard saw something move in the shadows along the other side of the wall. He saw what looked to be another form, the hands tied behind, a head drooping in sleep. The head moved slightly from side to side. In the dim light he caught sight of a strawberry blonde curl. Quickly moving back to the curve of the wall, he knew it was her. He'd found Kylin.

But how was he going to get her out? The entrance was fortified with more guards and he was sure Claec was in the cave somewhere possibly even Cadda. He was outnumbered and didn't even have a weapon to defend himself. The only way out of the cave was through the hole he had come through. This time he had to take Kylin with him and push her through before he could escape himself. He knew her smaller body would fit easier through the hole, but he couldn't tell if she was awake. He remembered Claec and Cadda talking in the dungeon and the mention of potions that were used. He was sure the way she was slumped over, she was still asleep, and daylight was quickly approaching.

He looked once more at the guard, then to the dirt. Moving down, his fingers ran over the dirt floor as he searched for any pebbles. He found three nice sized pebbles and clenched them in his hand. Moving up the cave wall, he looked to the guard who was now almost asleep from the way his head was down. Taking one of the pebbles, he threw it on the other side of the guard. The guard stirred but didn't awaken. He took the second pebble and threw it a little closer, so it fell next to him. The guard's head moved, and he heard a mumble from him. He took the third pebble and threw it down the cave a little farther. This time the guard woke up. He stood placing his hand on his sword.

"Who's there?" The guard walked toward the cave where he heard the sound. The guard looked to Kylin then took a couple more steps toward the sound. Aethelhard ran out from behind the cave wall. Surprised by the sudden attack, the guard dropped his sword. Aethelhard placed his hands firmly around the guard's neck so he wouldn't be able to make a sound. The guard's eyes became wild and he clawed at the hands that held him. Aethelhard pressed his hands tighter on his neck. The guard's struggling was now only a feeble attempt at gaining freedom. After a few more minutes, his eyes rolled back into his head and his body became limp.

Aethelhard let the guard's body fall silently onto the cave floor and looked toward the front of the cave. So far, so good. He picked up the sword and quickly walked to Kylin's slumped form. He brought up her tied hands and cut the ropes that bound her with the newly acquired sword. Her body was limp, her head rolling from side to side as he tried to wake her.

"Kylin. Kylin, can you hear me?"

Her eyes fluttered open for a moment, her lips moving slightly. He leaned his head closer to listen.

"Where are you going?"

Aethelhard looked up hearing a man's voice coming down the tunnel of the cave. He cursed softly and hoisted Kylin on his shoulder. It wouldn't be long until he was discovered. It would be slow going with him having to carry Kylin. He ran as quietly and quickly as he could. At least with Kylin in her present state, she wouldn't be much trouble.

"Here take this to him." Aethelhard heard the same man's voice call out. He heard the steps stop and then fade as the man walked back toward the entrance. At least he would have a few more minutes to get to the hole in the cave wall.

Finally reaching the hole, he took Kylin from his shoulder and pushed her feet first as gently as possible through the hole and onto the ground below.

"Milord, she's gone!"

"What?" Aethelhard recognized that voice as Quintrell's. "What do you mean she's gone?" He heard footsteps quickly moving down the tunnel now.

Quintrell looked at the guard on the ground and noticed his sword was gone. Looking down the cave tunnel, he whispered, "Aethelhard."

He let go of her hands so she would fall gently to the ground below. Not much time left, he thought. He could hear the footsteps running down the tunnel toward him.

"He must have found an entrance down here," Quintrell said.

Aethelhard hoisted himself up the wall toward the hole, his fingers grasping the top of the hole just as he saw Quintrell turn the corner.

"There he is!" He saw Quintrell's eyes narrow as he spoke through gritted teeth. "Kill him."

The guards ran toward him as he tried to push himself through the hole. Cursing softly as the sword caught between him and the rock wall. He grabbed the sword, pulling it out from his belt and slipped through the hole just as the guards started to grab for his feet. He heard the sword fall with a thud on the cave's dirt floor.

"Get him!" Quintrell yelled to the others.

One of the guards started to go through the hole just as Aethelhard picked up Kylin.

"What's taking so long?" Quintrell yelled.

"I'm stuck, milord," the guard shouted back.

Aethelhard turned back to see the man's body stuck and moving slightly back and forth as the men in the cave pulled and pushed on him. He turned and started through the thick underbrush with Kylin over his shoulder.

"Go out the entrance. Don't let him escape!" Aethelhard heard Quintrell's muffled words as he ran into the forest.

"Go that way," Quintrell's voice boomed.

If it had been just him, he could have easily slipped away but carrying Kylin make it a lot more difficult

He looked behind him. He did not see Quintrell or the guards but could tell from their voices and the hacking of the brush, they were not far behind.

The blush of a new morning was just starting to filter through the trees as he tripped over a vine on the ground. He fell, Kylin tumbling in front of him. He pulled his foot from the vine and panicked for a moment when he did not see her. The men were closing in. He did not have much time. Moving the low hanging branches of a tree, he saw her in a large hole partially covered by the vines. He looked behind him and jumped in beside her, pulling some of the vines and underbrush to hide them. He lay as flat and still as possible, his body over Kylin's to keep her still.

Quintrell stood breathless next to the branches of a tree nearby. Aethelhard did not dare breath for giving away their hiding spot. He felt Kylin shift under him and prayed she wouldn't wake now.

"He must be here somewhere," Quintrell said as he walked closer to the hole. "Move your swords through the bushes. He could not have gotten far with Kylin."

"Yes, milord," the guard said.

Aethelhard lay as still as he could, hearing the swords cutting away the vines and brush around them. Quintrell's sword broke through some of the branches over them only inches from where they lay.

"Keep searching," Quintrell said. "I will give the man who finds them fifty gold pieces, but I want Kylin alive."

Aethelhard heard the men's voices drifting through the brush as they started to move away. His heart was pounding in his chest. He knew it wouldn't be long until they returned this way back to the cave.

Aethelhard lay quietly listening for any signs that Quintrell and the guards were returning but all that he heard was Kylin's soft breathing. His mind raced as he tried to come up with a plan but even if they did escape, he'd have to take Kylin back to her father. He was not sure how Hutton would react to him being on the castle grounds much less with Kylin in tow. Kylin could tell him who kidnapped her and what happened, but he doubted if Hutton would believe her. He would think it was all a plan for Aethelhard to take his daughter.

As he lay thinking, he heard the creaking of wagon wheels. They must be near a road or clearing. A wagon would not be able to get through the thick underbrush or navigate along the bed of the stream. A road nearby could be a way of escape or it could be a way of capture. Quintrell could be positioned along the road waiting for him or even some of Hutton's knights. He heard the creaking slowing then finally stop. He lay still under the branches of the tree in the womb of the earth.

"Aethelhard," a woman's voice spoke softly.

He didn't answer and lay still thinking it must be a trick. Quintrell must have bribed a local woman to go along the road calling his name to find him.

"Aethelhard," the woman spoke a little louder. "Would get up here before someone sees us or suspicions are raised?"

Was that Laila's voice? His heart was pounding in his chest as he carefully pushed away some of the branches to see who was calling him. He saw an old woman wearing peasant clothes, a brown shawl covering her gray hair, her face old and wrinkled, yet there was something familiar about her. She was looking to where they were hiding. He looked down the road and over as much of the area as he could see without giving away their hiding place.

Laila hoped she was at the right place. She heard her sister's voice encouraging her to stay. She was at the right spot.

"Aethelhard, come out of that hole," she said.

He was now sure of the voice. It was Laila's but the old woman didn't look anything like her. He cautiously moved the branches and looked to her.

"Laila?" he asked curiously.

"Yes." She looked down the road then back to him. "Is Kylin with you?"

Aethelhard pulled himself from the hole. "Yes." He looked to her face, his brow furrowing for a moment.

"Hurry. Before we are seen." Laila pulled back the blanket that was covering the straw to keep it from being blown off the wagon by the wind. "Bring Kylin and get under here."

Aethelhard looked over the forest once more, then picked up Kylin and carried her to the wagon.

"Is she dead?"

Aethelhard gently placed her in the straw. Kylin moved a little, a soft sound escaping her lips. "She was given a sleeping potion."

"By whom?"

"Geary made the potion but Claec made sure she drank it." Aethelhard looked into Laila's face and saw her eyes burning with rage. There was no doubt in his mind that this was Laila. "How did you find us?"

Laila looked away for a moment then turned her eyes back to him. "I have my ways."

Aethelhard picked up Kylin and sat on the wagon laying down in the straw.

"We must hurry," Laila said as she pulled the blanket over the two. "Claec must be thinking of a plan as we speak. We must get to the castle before him if we are to have a chance of the truth being told."

Aethelhard heard the snap of the ropes on the horses and the wagon creaked then slowly started to move. Kylin stirred as well, her eyes opening and a look of panic when she saw the blanket over them. He grabbed her hands and covered her mouth as he moved close to her.

"Kylin, it's Aethelhard," he whispered.

She looked to him, her eyes trying to focus in the confusion that filled her mind. "Aethelhard?" She spoke just loud enough for him to hear.

"Yes, Kylin."

"Where are we?" There was still panic in her voice. They were moving through the village. He did not want to risk her becoming coherent and trying to jump from the wagon.

"In a wagon. Your mother is leading the wagon home."

She started to call to her mother but Aethelhard pressed his hand over her lips.

"Shh, it's too dangerous right now. We need to wait until she tells us it is safe."

Kylin looked to him, her mind still spinning from the potion. "I'm scared."

Aethelhard moved closer to her and cradled her in his arms. "It is all right, Kylin. I won't let anything happen to you."

Kylin's body relaxed and moved closer to him. He brushed a stray curl from her eyes listening once more to her soft breathing.

The faint noises in the village grew louder and soon filled the air around them. He heard men shouting and women gathering their children close to them. A dog chased the wagon for a while, then the sound of chickens and goats was heard. The chaos around them started to fade until all he heard was the creaking of the wheels as the wagon continued its journey.

The horse's feet clopped on the wood as they crossed a bridge, the wagon's wheels moaning in quiet song. The village behind them, the sounds of the castle started becoming louder.

"Halt!"

The wagon slowed to a stop.

"Who are you and what is your business with Milord's castle," the knight said as he moved closer to the wagon.

"I am Lady D'arcy and my business is the castle," Laila said firmly removing the shawl that covered her head.

The knight bowed then looked at her curiously with her peasant clothes. "I am sorry, Milady D'arcy. I didn't recognize you."

The ropes once more snapped and the horses started on their way across the bridge. When the wagon stopped, Aethelhard lifted a corner of the blanket to see they were in a small alcove next to the keep. The wagon shifted as Laila got off. She looked over the grounds to make sure they were hidden then lifted the blanket. She looked to Kylin who was still cradled in Aethelhard's arms.

"Can she walk?" Laila asked.

"She's still a little drowsy, but I think we can make it," Aethelhard said.

Laila looked around and nodded. "We must hurry."

Aethelhard jumped down from the wagon and helped Kylin to her feet. She was still a little unsettled but was awake enough to walk.

Laila turned toward the ivy that grew along the castle wall and pushed on a large stone revealing a tunnel that went through the walls inside the keep. "Follow me and do not make a sound."

Aethelhard nudged Kylin toward the tunnel. Once inside, Kylin seemed to be more alert, her footsteps becoming easier with each step. Laila closed the stone and waited for her eyes to adjust to the dim light. There were cracks in the outer wall that let in bits of light. Laila motioned them as she started down the tunnel. Quietly they crept along the dark walls. Aethelhard had placed Kylin between him and Laila just in case she stumbled so he could catch her.

Ahead he saw light coming from one side of the wall. It was here that Laila paused, her fingers moving lightly over the stones. They stopped for only a moment and a soft click was heard before the stones rotated.

Hutton hearing the click from the wall as well quickly pulled his sword out not knowing who could have found the secret tunnel to his chamber. Aethelhard, Kylin, Claec and now it seemed, even his wife was missing. It was as if they were disappearing one by one in front of his eyes.

Laila stepped from the tunnel.

"Laila, it's you," Hutton said relieved. He then saw Kylin emerge from the tunnel. "You found Kylin too? Do you know who took her? I will have his head once I get my hands on him." Anger shot from his eyes as he inspected Kylin making sure she was not harmed.

"Yes," Laila said as she walked to Hutton's side.

Hutton started to move toward the stones to close them but Aethelhard stepped from the tunnel as well.

"You traitor!" Hutton said as his eyes filled with rage. He turned to call Cadda when Laila grabbed his beard and held tightly to it.

"Quiet! It was Aethelhard, who saved your daughter," Laila spoke firmly to him.

Hutton looked to Aethelhard, then back to Laila.

"It is Claec who kidnapped Kylin and made it look as if Aethelhard did it," Laila said.

"Claec was kidnapped as well or killed for all I know." Hutton looked to Aethelhard his hand moving to his sword.

Laila released Hutton and walked in front of Aethelhard. "You'll kill me first."

"Father, she's right," Kylin said. "Claec is behind all of this. He only wanted to marry me to have control over your land then Aethelhard's. He is not who he says he is."

Hutton laughed. "Do you not think I know who he is? He is Lord Garrett Quintrell's son. I have known Garrett for many years."

"But did you ever meet his son?" Laila said.

Hutton stopped and looked at her, his fingers moving gingerly over his recently pulled beard. "No, I don't believe I have seen him since he was a boy."

"He's a man now," Laila said. "How do you know that the man portraying Claec is actually his son? Garrett and his son were called by the King to help fight the Scots. They could both be dead now."

Hutton sat down as the whole situation started to weigh on him. He ran a hand through his hair, then stood defiantly. "No! I don't have traitors among my own people."

"You called Aethelhard a traitor and yet you still vowed to help him. How's that different? In your own eyes, you have felt traitors on your land, but you didn't know who." Laila stepped toward him as she spoke.

Hutton looked to them again, his face becoming tense. "Enough! Geary!"

Geary shuffled into the chamber.

"Yes, milord," he bowed. When he stood and saw Aethelhard and Kylin, his face became panicked. He turned and walked quickly into the hallway.

"Cadda!" Hutton's voice boomed.

A knight ran into the room. "Cadda has not returned from the village, milord."

"Find and capture Geary. Put him in the dungeon. No one is to see him unless I am in attendance as well."

The knight hurried out of the room to find Geary.

"Cadda is involved as well, father," Kylin said. "He helped Claec with everything."

Hutton spun around. "What?"

"I saw him in the cave where I found Kylin," Aethelhard said. "I also heard him, Claec, and Geary talking in the dungeon while I was captive."

Hutton started to pace the floor. "Is it not enough to have one traitor? Must I have three?" He stopped and drew his sword into the air. "I'll have all of their heads on my castle wall as a warning to others who would even think of betraying me."

A knight came back into the chamber. "Milord?"

Hutton turned toward the knight his sword drawn. "Yes?"

The knight took a step back and bowed. "Geary is in the dungeon as you commanded."

"Put two knights around his cell to guard him."

"Yes, milord," the knight said and disappeared out of the chamber.

Hutton followed the knight as well.

The light turned to darkness with only candles for light in Laila's chamber. She sat at the small table brushing her long hair. Supper had long past and she had not seen Hutton. She looked through the glass that reflected her image as she went over the day's events. At least Kylin was safe and in her own chamber this eve. Aethelhard had also excused himself after supper to rest. It was to be expected. Both had been through a harrowing experience and the rest would do them good. Still…there had been no word of Claec or Cadda. It was as if both had disappeared without a clue. The cave had been thoroughly searched as well as the woods. She turned her head as Hutton entered their chambers. His face was strained; his clothes torn and muddy.

"Did you find them?" Laila asked as she put down her brush.

"No."

She walked to the curtained bed. "What have you decided to do with Geary."

"Nothing." Hutton put his sword down and started to remove his muddy clothes.

"I thought you were going to punish him," Laila said pulling the warmed blankets over her.

"I can't."

She propped up a pillow to sit against. "He was your servant."

Hutton said nothing as he continued to prepare for bed. After he joined his wife, he finally spoke. "He's dead…poisoned most likely." He turned to the candle and blew it out.

Chapter 5

Hutton got up from his restless sleep as soon as there was light. He put on his clothes, quietly closed the chamber door, then went to the dining room for mead and something to eat. He drank his mead quickly taking the honeyed bread with him then spotted the steward. He walked quicker but not quick enough.

"Milord, we must talk," the steward said as he continued to annoy Hutton as much as the bee which buzzed around his honeyed bread.

"Not now," Hutton said firmly. He kept walking across the grounds toward the stables.

"But, milord, there are urgent matters of the village that demand your attention."

Hutton stopped and the steward almost ran into him. The steward continued. "There are urgent matters, that are concerned with disagreements over land, rent, and payments." Hutton ignored him and looked toward the stables finally finding the one he was seeking.

"Reese." A knight by the stables stopped talking and walked over to Hutton.

"Yes, milord," Reese said.

"Have you found Cadda or Lord Quintrell?"

"No, milord. We have searched the grounds, the forest, and the cave. There's no sign of either. The knights and I were discussing where else to continue our search."

Hutton looked to the knights by the stable then to Reese. "Carry on and let me know when you find them."

"Yes, milord," Reese bowed and returned to the other knights.

The steward never left Hutton's side. He waited for his chance once more to reiterate the importance of his business. "Milord, if I may have a few minutes of your time."

Hutton stopped and looked toward the sky. His hands raised, he looked back to the steward. "What is it? What is so important it can not wait until another day?"

The steward stopped and started to sift through the pages he was carrying. "There are many things. One man accused of stealing another's pig, rents to be collected from the surrounding land, many papers to sign, and just last eve there was damage to the inn by a drunken man."

Hutton continued to walk toward the main hall. "I have other things that I must tend to today."

"But milord," the steward pressed. "The one who damaged the inn wishes to continue on his journey. He's willing to pay for all damages and the fine with cash he has with him."

Hutton stopped. "Have you seen what this man looks like?"

"Yes, milord. He looks as if he's a rogue and always wears the hood of his cloak close to his face."

"Did you get a good look at his face?" Hutton looked toward town, his fingers moving slowly over his beard.

The steward looked to him puzzled. "No, milord. But I did see his gold pieces."

"Gold pieces," Hutton repeated slowly. "You didn't find it out of the ordinary that a rogue would be carrying bags of gold coins?" Hutton was now looking intently toward the village.

"Some men carry large sums of money when they travel." The steward was once again sifting through the papers he was holding.

"Bring him to me," Hutton said as he approached the main hall.

"Bring him to you?" The steward questioned.

Hutton turned toward the steward. "Take Reese with you."

The steward looked to him confused as Hutton walked into the main hall. "As you wish, milord."

Hutton saw Aethelhard at the large table as he walked inside. "Were you able to get the maps?" Hutton poured a mug of mead as he spoke.

"Yes. They were with the other records as you said."

Hutton sat down and looked over them. "Did you see any weaknesses?"

"The castle is protected especially with the fortifications you recently made. Although there is a place here that could be a way to the upper castle grounds."

Hutton looked over the map and then sat back in his chair trying to picture the spot that Aethelhard had pointed out. "If there is a weakness, we'll have to fortify it before we leave. I'll be taking most of my men with me to get control of Elwyn Castle. I can't leave Nottes Castle unprotected with my wife and daughter here especially with Cadda still loose. He knows the castle as well as I do." Hutton thoughtfully brought his fingers to his chin as he thought for a moment. "Maybe even better. He was my best knight. He guarded the castle well and will know of every weakness." Hutton looked out the window of the hall and toward the village, his fist suddenly coming down hard on the rough table. "The castle must be completely fortified. Everything must be checked thoroughly. If there is a weakness, Cadda will know it."

Aethelhard started to roll up the maps. "Then we'll have to look over the castle on foot. Stone by stone, we'll check the outer wall for any passages."

"Agreed," Hutton said. He walked over to the large hearth that stood at the end of the room. The ashes were smoldering, and wisps of smoke trailed up through the chimney.

A servant came into the room setting down a bucket of water and towels. He placed the towels in the water that smelled of lye and wiped the towels over the stone floor. Hutton paced by the hearth for a few moments, then looked up. "Get Reese. He is to report to me here at once."

The servant looked up from his chore of cleaning the floor. A towel was dripping water on the floor and he quickly wiped it away before standing and bowing. "Yes, milord." He quickly left through the door leaving the bucket next to the table; the towels strewn close by.

Reese entered the room a few minutes later and bowed his head. "Yes, milord. You wished to see me?"

Hutton nodded, his foot lightly kicking the stone ledge that led to the hearth. "I need for you and the other knights to go around the castle wall. Check every stone. Look for any weaknesses in the wall. Also look for anything that might be a tunnel. You will also need to check all the weapons. Make sure all blades are honed to a sharp edge. All trebuchets and other defenses must be in working order. Those we do not take with us may also be called for battle here. I feel that Cadda isn't gone."

"Would you still like for me to go into the village with the steward?" Reese questioned.

Hutton thought for a moment. "No, the fortification of the castle comes first. Tell the steward to collect money for the damages and the man's fines. He can be released after all debts have been paid."

Aethelhard looked out the window and saw the sun slowly sinking in the sky. The warmth of the day was fading, and a light breeze was moving the leaves of the trees outside the window. "When will we leave for Elwyn castle?" Aethelhard asked emotionless.

"As soon as everything has been fortified and the men and weapons are ready. Reese should have the fortifications completed and the perimeter checked before the sun sets tomorrow. We need to move quickly before the opportunity is lost. If we leave at dark tomorrow, we should be at the castle by nightfall the next day. This will give us at least a little protection."

"How do you plan on getting into the castle?"

"It is your castle," Hutton said. "You're the one who knows its defenses and weaknesses. What's your plan?"

Aethelhard walked toward the window and looked out again. Activity was all around him as the men scurried to complete their tasks. He turned from the window and walked to the worn table, lifting his booted foot on the rung of a chair. "I think we use the trebuchets on the opposite side of the castle from the stream. This will distract the men and bring most of them to that side of the castle. I'll be able to slip under the waterfall and through the tunnel that leads next to the guard tower. There will be one maybe two guards in the towers. I will overcome them myself and lower the drawbridge for the others to enter the castle grounds. It will not take many men to operate the trebuchets. With the forest somewhat shielding them, it will be difficult for Blackmon and his men to know how many men are actually there."

Hutton nodded his eyes not moving from the hearth. His fingers moved over his chin of thick course hair. "How many men will we be able to get through the tunnel and inside?"

"I'll go through the tunnel myself. The other men will stay outside until the drawbridge is lowered."

"Are there any defenses over the drawbridge?" Hutton walked slowly in front of the hearth.

Aethelhard thought for moment. "Only arrow slips from the wall that connects the two guard towers. If I kill the men in the tower, that will take care of any other traps."

"There's no other place they will be able to pour boiling oil or water?"

"No."

Hutton turned toward the table and picked up his mug of mead. "How many entrances to the towers?"

"One stairwell each with the connecting wall between them."

Hutton thought momentarily as he finished his mead. "We'll leave tomorrow night. We will siege the castle under the darkness of night."

Hutton went with Reese to check every entrance of the wall with Reese. The men filled in cracks and replaced stones as needed. It was very late when Hutton made it back to his chamber. Laila was fast asleep and barely moved as he slipped under the warm skins. He slept for a few hours and was up before Laila stirred. He made his way to the kitchen to get some hot mead and bread before he headed out. Aethelhard was already at work before Hutton made it to the stables.

"Up rather early too," Hutton said to him.

Aethelhard looked up from the honing stone. "There is still much to do." The grinding started again when he went back to honing his sword and knives.

Hutton went out to find Reese who was with the trebuchets and ramming logs.

"Will everything be ready by nightfall?"

"Yes, milord. The castle and walls are secured. We will have all the men and weapons ready to leave by nightfall."

It took most of the day to ready everything. Just as the sun's long rays were touching the horizon, they set out for the long trip to Elwyn castle. All through the night then made slow but steady progress.

Hutton stopped everyone at dawn to eat and rest for a short time. They made better progress than he thought. The rain didn't come but the air was cooler with a slight breeze.

Aethelhard chewed absently on his bread going over all the preparations they made before leaving Nottes castle. They left a few men to guard the castle, Laila, and Kylin. He only hoped it would be enough.

As they approached Elwyn castle there was still an hour or two of light left. Aethelhard placed all the men and trebuchets by the woods giving them a few hours of rest. He then took some men with him to attack the other side of the castle. They were in position at dusk waiting for the attack to begin.

Screams were heard as the trebuchet threw its fiery load of hot coals within the castle wall. The stench of burning human flesh and blood was heavy in the air.

Aethelhard moved silently through the forests to the other side of the castle wall. He motioned the men to hold up as he slipped around a large rock and looked toward the castle. The twin towers stood black against the glow of battle and barrage of arrows behind them. He waited for a few more minutes, then saw someone move to the window of one of the towers. It would be a little tricky. He didn't think there would be many men at this position of the castle, but it only took one to kill especially from that vantagepoint. He looked over the stream that flowed from the castle and down the smooth rocks toward the forest. He moved away from the rock and felt something whiz past him. He lay flat against the rock as beads of sweat broke out on his forehead. He had not expected that. Blackmon must have men around the waterfall. Aethelhard looked toward the other side of the castle where the battle raged on.

Hutton turned behind him hearing a scream and watched as another one of his men went down under a barrage of arrows. The thick black smoke from the dry brush burning under the wall was offering some cover but not near enough. A large boulder flew hitting the wall just above the fire and some of the stones of the wall shifted. Hutton turned toward the other side of the castle and hoped Aethelhard was having better luck than he was.

"There are guards by the stream," he told the men. "Blackmon must have expected us to come this way with the battle on the other side of the castle. I'll get to the waterfall and inside the castle to lower the drawbridge. If I do not return within an hour, you are to join Hutton and continue the battle."

"But milord, shouldn't you take one of us with you? What if you need help?" one of the knights asked.

"I'll go with you," Reese said.

"No. I'll do this alone. It will be harder for them to spot one person than two."

Reese started to say something more but seeing the determined look in Aethelhard's eyes wisely decided not to continue the discussion. "Yes, milord."

Aethelhard checked his weapons, then pointed toward the drawbridge. "Get as close as you can to the drawbridge without being seen and as soon as it's lowered, storm the castle."

Aethelhard made his way back to the large boulder. He looked around then took an arrow from his quiver. Taking aim, he shot it toward the trees on the other side of the stream. A flock of birds sitting on a nearby limb flew through the low hanging branches and into the sky. As the birds flew past the branches, Aethelhard looked from the other side of the boulder and saw a single guard; his eyes glued to the arrow as it went through the trees.

The guard continued to watch the trees. He took another step closer to the trees and pulled out another arrow. The guard was sure that the enemy was in the trees. A muffled scream was all that pierced the air. Aethelhard looked at the dead man as he took his weapons. He then took the dead man's clothes and armor leaving the naked man in a growing pool of blood.

Aethelhard pulled the helmet over his face and looked toward the tower. The guard in the tower must have grown suspicious. Aethelhard stood up and waved to the tower guard. The guard waved back and moved away from the window.

Aethelhard felt the sweat pouring down his back as he made his way back toward the waterfall and the passage. At least with the dead man's clothing and armor, he'd be able to move about easier once inside.

He moved slowly toward the passageway. The wet damp air felt good as he made his way behind the waterfall. Everything was coming back to him as he moved quietly over the moss-covered rocks. He started to take another step then stopped. Crouching down, he looked at the moss on the rocks. The moss was still green and undisturbed. He looked up and smiled. Blackmon hadn't found the passageway after all. He had men posted by the waterfall because of the cover of the rocks but the undisturbed moss told him this passageway was still safe.

He walked between two large rocks then waited for his eyes to adjust to the darkness. His heavy boots scooted across the slippery moss as strong fingers felt along the stone wall. The crevasse should be about—here! He pressed between the large smooth slate rocks realizing how long it had been since he was here. What he remembered as an easy slip between the rocks as a child was now a struggle especially with the armor. He planted his foot on the slippery moss and pushed. His body moved slightly between the rocks but now he was stuck. He closed his eyes and took as deep of a breath as he could and pushed once more. His body slipped through the rocks and he stumbled into the chamber that was on the other side. He waited crouched, looking through the gloomy darkness, listening.

After a few minutes, he continued his journey though the darkness. As he felt along the walls toward the towers, he remembered how he had walked through a similar passageway in Hutton's castle. It was different then. Laila and Kylin had been with him. He remembered how her body felt next to his. The warmth he felt just being next to her.

His boot hit a rock and he stumbled again, cursing softly under his breath. That's what he got for thinking of women at a time like this. But it wasn't women; it was one woman who kept entering his mind. The girl he played tag with so many years ago around this waterfall was now a beautiful woman. He brushed himself off mumbling. She was also the same woman who almost got him killed…several times.

He moved slowly around a bend in the rocks. The damp stale air of the passageway was slowly being replaced with fresh air. The stone wall was ending, and a dirt wall was starting to replace it. He kept moving through the passageway until he came to the full dirt wall. The end of the passageway was at the top of the dirt tunnel. He would have to climb up the dirt tunnel to the entrance.

The tunnel going up was also narrower than he remembered. As a boy he had slid down the tunnel. Now he could place his knees and feet along the tunnel and push him self up. The dirt was loose in some places but remained packed overall. Finally, he saw the night sky above him.

He stuck the toes of his boots into the dirt walls and cautiously lifted his head above the hole. A light wind was stirring over the ground as he looked toward the other side of the castle where the battle raged.

"Keep those rocks flying," yelled Hutton. He saw his men dropping like ripened fruit in a strong wind, but they had to keep going. Another large boulder flew into the stone wall. The stones started to crumble under the constant pounding of the boulders and the fire that raged under it. Hutton saw a couple of the smaller stones fall into the raging hell which was consuming the wall.

"Get ready men. It won't be long now," he yelled over the thundering boulders and roar of the fire. Sparks coming from the fire below caught his eye and he watched as a few more of the stone blocks started to crumble. The men who were at the top of the wall had also noticed and started to move toward the sturdier parts of the wall. He looked toward the towers, then strained not believing what he saw. "He made it," Hutton smiled. "He actually made it."

The drawbridge clamored down as Aethelhard released the heavy chains. A loud thud signaled to the knights waiting nearby that the drawbridge and towers were secured. The knights ran quickly over the drawbridge and into the castle.

Aethelhard pulled his sword. "This way." Another man lay dead obscured by the shadows.

"He's dead," one of the knights said. "It is a trap."

The knights pulled their weapons and started to attack Aethelhard.

"What are you doing?" Aethelhard's sword clashed with one of the knight's swords.

"Look for any others," the knight yelled as he sliced his sword toward Aethelhard.

"Wait! It's me, Aethelhard!" He said as his sword stopped the knight's blow.

The knight stopped but still held his sword in a guarded position. "Show yourself," he demanded of Aethelhard.

Aethelhard threw down the helmet.

The knight dropped his sword to his side. "Milord. I thought it was you lying dead in the shadows."

Aethelhard cursed softly and kicked the helmet. "As will the others when they see me."

The knight standing in front of him screamed and fell forward into him. Aethelhard saw the arrow in his back. He looked up and saw the enemy scrambling across the wall toward them. His knights were scattering; he had to think fast. Quickly he let the knight fall and picked up the nearby helmet. After he placed it on his head, he waved toward the six or seven men on the wall. Too many for him to fight alone but if he could think of a plan with the knights, it was quite doable. He doubled back to the knights.

The knights who had hidden close by the wall grabbed their weapons quickly after hearing footsteps close by.

"It's Aethelhard," he said quietly.

"Show yourself," one of the knights said. Apparently, they were not going to be easily fooled. That was good. Aethelhard looked to the wall and quickly raised his helmet showing his face to the knights on the ground. He quickly placed it back on and joined the men by the wall.

"There are only six or seven men on the wall. The rest must still be fighting on the other side of the castle grounds." Aethelhard crouched down and started to draw in the soft dirt with the tip of his finger. "They think I am one of them, so we'll use this to our advantage." He drew out the plan in the dirt, then scooted his boot over to destroy the etchings. "Ready?" He looked to the men and stepped out of the shadows toward the tower.

He climbed the stairs toward the wall; beads of sweat once more starting to cover his forehead. If he failed, he would die. He was sure of that. But he would rather die defending his castle than to concede and let Blackmon have control of it. He opened the door leading out to the wall that was between the towers. The men quickly went into a defensive posture only to relax as they saw it was one of their own.

The men were scattered over the wall, a couple here and some alone but their eyes were constantly searching the grounds. Aethelhard looked around for something that would cause a distraction.

A loud noise was heard as heavy blocks of stone gave way. Sparks and flames filled the dark sky and screams of men falling into the great hell below were heard. Aethelhard looked toward the far wall.

"One more boulder," yelled Hutton. "That should bring the wall down."

The men heaved and pushed another boulder onto the waiting trebuchet. A nearby scream heard from the knight who was waiting to cut the rope for the trebuchet to throw its deadly load. Hutton looked around and saw the enemy swarming his knights. The clashing of swords, moans from the dying, and screams from those who were lucky enough to die quickly. His sword clashed against another as the man charged him. Taking the great sword into two hands, he dealt a mighty blow causing the man to almost drop his sword. Quickly Hutton moved his sword decapitating the man.

Hutton ran toward the trebuchet. It was their only hope to enter the castle. He raised his heavy sword just feet from the trebuchet only to feel a sharp pain in his leg.

Turning, he saw the bloody sword, anger filling his eyes. His sword already brought up, he let if fall with a deafening bow onto the man's shoulder causing his arm to nearly severe from his body. Hutton looked toward the trebuchet and dragging his injured leg was finally able to cut the rope that sent the boulder sailing toward the wall.

The wall groaned against the heavy assault. The large stones moving a little more and then the wall started to fall. First one stone, then two the great structure's integrities at last failing. The stones fell into the great caldron of fire that burned under the wall. The heated air was alive with sparks. The flames licked up the stones of the wall and Hutton watched as they quickly spread over the top of the wall igniting the source of energy. A caldron of heated oil exploded with flames, then fell behind the wall, the air resonating with screams, the smell of burning human flesh quickly filling his nostrils.

Aethelhard watched as the spectacle unfolded. The castle wall fell. The screams of the men dying were faint, but the smell of human flesh was strong. At least there was a distraction. The knights made their way to the top of the towers. Aethelhard raised his sword and they attacked.

The men were stunned as one of their own raked his sword across the man's chest. The man fell to the ground, writhing in pain, his blood soon covering the stones. Aethelhard kicked the dying man away and went after another. The clashing of weapons mixed with the faint sound of battle from the other side of the castle. Aethelhard's eyes darted over the wall and saw a man with his sword closing in on one of his knights. He ran toward the man and slammed his sword into the man's skull. The man staggered and Aethelhard pushed him over the wall. His screams silenced as his body collided with the ground below. Breathing hard, Aethelhard grabbed the knight's hand pulling him from the wall. They gathered by one of the towers catching their breath.

"Any dead," Aethelhard said between heavy gulps of air.

"Only one," one of the knights said.

"Where is he?" Aethelhard looked over the wall.

"Over there," the knight pointed.

Aethelhard walked toward the knight leaving a trail of the clothes he was wearing. He took the bloody clothes and armor from the knight. The dead man's body already becoming cold on the gray stone. Aethelhard put the clothes and armor on and hooked his head toward the battle that raged behind them. "Let's go."

Hutton took off the scarf his wife had given him for good luck. He hated to use it in this way but if there was ever a time, he needed good luck it was now. He wrapped the scarf around his leg, tying the cloth tightly to stop the flow of blood. He grimaced as he stood on the injured leg.

"Milord, you are injured," one of the knights said as the battle ensured around them.

"I might be injured but I'm not dead," growled Hutton. At least not yet, he thought to himself. He ignored the pain in his leg and picked up his sword. "We've a battle to win." Hutton charged through the breach in the castle wall away from the fire and toward the battle that awaited him inside the castle.

The first light of day touched the horizon with colors of red and gold. Aethelhard looked over the slaughter that lay before him. Still breathing hard, he leaned over, letting his sword touch the ground for the first time in hours.

"Aethelhard."

He looked up and saw Hutton limping toward him with Laila's scarf wrapped around his leg.

"How bad are you hurt?" Aethelhard said as he sat on the ground, the faint moans of a man who had not yet died drifting past them.

"Not bad," Hutton said as he looked to his leg. "Hurt like the devil at first but seemed to hurt less the more I fought." Hutton sat down next to Aethelhard, placing his injured leg out straight in front of him.

"Let's see how deep it is," said Aethelhard.

"Looks like you took quite a blood bath yourself," Hutton said.

Aethelhard started to unwrap the scarf. "Just a few scratches." He took the bloody scarf from Hutton's leg and tossed it to him. "Might still need this."

Hutton wrapped the scarf around his neck as he looked at his leg. "How bad is it?"

Aethelhard crouched looking over his leg. His brows furrowed as he moved the bloody clothing from him. "Are you sure you were injured?"

"I may not know a lot of things, but I do know what a sword feels like in my leg," Hutton sat up to get a closer look at his leg. "There's only dried blood." He smiled silently thanking Laila. "There's blood all over me as well, but I'm not injured."

Aethelhard sat down on the ground and leaned against a large stone that had fallen from the wall.

Hutton gingerly moved his leg. "It's still sore. The sword must have grazed it. Laila's good luck scarf worked." He smiled, running his fingers over the scarf.

"Milord!" A boy came running toward them stepping around the dead bodies which littered the ground. When he reached the two, he bowed. "Milords, I have distressing news."

"What is it?" Hutton said as he turned toward the boy. Aethelhard recognized him as one of the squires who was in training. His clothes were now torn, dirty and his hair was matted. Aethelhard looked closer at the boy's head and saw it was blood that matted his hair.

"The castle, milord. It's under attack."

"What?" Hutton struggled to stand. "By whom?"

The squire looked to Hutton then bowed his head speaking softly. "Cadda."

Hutton's eyes filled with hatred. "Who? Speak up."

The boy looked at Hutton in fear. "Cadda and another man I did not know."

Hutton cursed trying to stand on his injured leg. "Where's my horse?"

"You'll never make the journey," Aethelhard stood and picked up his sword.

"The hell I won't," Hutton shot back in anger.

"Stay here. Bury the dead and start the rebuilding of the castle wall. I'll take the knights and go back," Aethelhard said.

Hutton looked back to the squire. "What about Laila and Kylin?"

"I don't know, milord. No one has seen them since the attack. It's said they are being held captive in the keep."

Hutton cursed again and slammed his sword into the ground. "I have to go back."

"No," Aethelhard sternly answered. "With your injuries you'll not be able to fight. There are already enough dead men. I don't want to be responsible for your death as well. The people in the village will help you now." Aethelhard started to walk away from them.

"Aethelhard."

He paused and turned toward Hutton. "Yes."

"Good luck."

Aethelhard quickly gathered the knights that were left. There was no time to bring the heavier weapons. If Laila and Kylin were being held captive, they had to get there quickly. They could even be dead by now. His anger grew as he thought of Kylin lying dead in a pool of blood. He dug his heels into his steed riding him harder than he had ever done before. They rode hard through the day and just as the sun was starting to set, the castle came into view.

Aethelhard slowed his steed looking for a place to hide until darkness. The cave would be risky since Cadda already knew about it. He looked toward the forest where the cave was. Maybe it was the perfect place to hide since it was the most obvious. Cadda may not expect them to use it.

He dismounted his steed and handed the reins to Reese. "I'm going to scout for a place to hide. If I'm not back by sunrise, take the men and return to Elwyn castle."

"Yes, milord," Reese said as he took the steed's reins.

Aethelhard disappeared into the thick foliage toward the cave. He crept quietly through the trees staying as hidden as possible. Cadda could have secured the cave but since he was in the castle, he may not have thought about it. He heard the stream and the faint smell of water. He was close.

Soft grass covered shape of the cave. He crawled on his belly to reach the hole he found earlier. He stayed still for a few minutes, listening for any sounds. He thought about the first time he came here and how the sound of the stream had almost lulled him to sleep. Now it sounded like torrent rain in his ears, disguising any other sounds that might be a warning to others close by. He thought of Kylin. The bitterness of his anger churning in his stomach burning as it moved up his throat. The anger threatened to overtake him, he shook it off as he moved slowly to the hole and peered inside the darkness. The cave appeared to be abandoned.

He squeezed through the hole and landed in the soft dirt. He waited for his eyes to adjust to the darkness then followed the damp walls around the cave, pausing for a moment as he came to the place where he had rescued Kylin. He moved to the mouth of the cave just as the long shadows of night were filtering through the thick trees. Satisfied they would be safe here, he returned with the knights.

The horses were drinking from the stream. They'd gathered grass for the horses to eat inside the cave. Aethelhard sat down with the knights and chewed on some dried meat.

"How many do you think are in the castle?" One of the knights said finally breaking the silence.

They were all tired and Aethelhard knew they should wait for the attack, but he couldn't. The anger in the pit of his stomach kept burning as he thought of what Cadda and Claec were doing to Kylin and Laila. He was sure the other man the squire spoke of was Claec. Neither was seen or killed in the battle at Elwyn castle. The knights would have recognized either of them.

"I'm not sure," he finally said. "Probably not many considering the number of men at Elwyn castle. It could just be Cadda and Claec. Cadda knows of every passageway into the castle."

"Kylin and Laila could already be dead."

Aethelhard's hand flew out before he realized it and landed a punch to the man's jaw. "Don't ever say that again in my presence."

The other men fell silent, quickly going back to what they were doing.

"Yes milord," the knight said as he rubbed his jaw.

Aethelhard walked away from the others running his fingers roughly through his hair. Tension was high especially with little rest after the lengthy battle the night before then the ride here. They had little to eat and knew even less of what they faced to rescue Laila and Kylin. He sat on a large rock next to a boulder not sure what to do.

Aethelhard jumped as the rock shifted. He furrowed his brows, then kicked at the dirt that was under the large rock, moving slowly around to where the rock and boulder touched. It was here that the ground gave in just a little. He placed his foot next to the boulder and with all his weight stepped on the dirt. The dirt moved under his foot causing the boulder to shift.

"What the…" Reese grabbed Aethelhard's shoulders and quickly pulled him from the tilting boulder. "What are you trying to do? Kill yourself?"

Aethelhard scrambled back toward the boulder and started to dig around it. Reese grabbed his shoulders and pulled him back again. "Have you gone mad?" Aethelhard elbowed him and Reese fell to the ground. "What are you doing?"

"Quick, get the men. I've found our way inside the castle." Aethelhard was digging frantically around the boulder. His fingers slipping through a small opening between the dirt and the boulder. He felt fresh air. The boulder started to shift toward him. Two of the knights leaned against it to keep it from moving more.

Reese looked at the boulder then to Aethelhard. "What's under the boulder?"

"I'm not sure. It could be a tunnel. The earth under the boulder is soft. I was able to move it away and slip my fingers between the dirt and the boulder." Aethelhard looked where he'd been digging.

"Even if there's a tunnel under there, how are we going to move that boulder? It would crush us all," Reese said as he looked at the two men moving away from the boulder.

"If we move enough of the dirt the weight of the boulder will cause it to fall toward the hole we created. This should expose the tunnel."

Reese looked at Aethelhard curiously. "Even if we survive, the boulder could fall toward the entrance and bury it…if there's a tunnel."

Aethelhard turned and looked to Reese. "Do you have a way into the castle?"

Reese took a deep resigned breath and shook his head.

"We've got to try," Aethelhard said.

Some of the knights leaned against the heavy boulder to keep it from falling while the others dug quickly. The knights grunted against the heavy boulder as it shifted toward the created hole.

"Now! Move!" Aethelhard shouted. Everyone moved, the boulder teetered a moment before falling away from the tunnel with a loud crash into nearby trees. They all stood motionless.

"It's a small hole," Reese said as they looked over it.

Aethelhard crouched down and started to dig again. "We'll have to move more of the dirt."

"But the boulder could shift and slide down the tunnel killing us," Reese said.

"It's a chance I'm willing to take to save Laila and Kylin," Aethelhard said.

Reese and the others started to dig, keeping a wary eye on the boulder that at any moment could slide down and kill them. Finally, the hole was large enough and Aethelhard dropped down into the cavern below.

"What does it look like?" Reese peered through the hole.

"It's a tunnel," Aethelhard said as he cautiously stepped deeper into the cavern. "Get me a torch."

Reese handed a torch to him. "See anything?" He waited, keeping his distance in case the boulder started to fall. After not hearing anything, he reluctantly laid on his belly on the ground next to the hole. "Aethelhard." He heard faint steps coming from the tunnel but Aethelhard didn't answer. "Get your weapons ready, men." After a few minutes Reese made out the faint light of the torch as someone was approaching in the cavern. "Aethelhard." He waited cautiously for a reply. The light from the torch moving closer. Aethelhard finally emerged from the cavern. Reese readied his weapon in case he wasn't alone.

"It's a tunnel," Aethelhard said as he came back into view.

"Where does it lead?"

"It appears to lead back to the castle," Aethelhard looked up at Reese.

Reese looked toward the boulder then shook his head. "If we die, we die together." Reese jumped down into the cavern with the other knights following close behind. Aethelhard started down the tunnel, the torch casting eerie shadows of the men as they walked further into the bowels of the earth.

Chapter 6

"Mother, what will happen to us?" Kylin whispered so the guard standing close could not hear.

"It'll be fine," Laila tried to smile reassuring. She held her daughter close and gently caressed her hair.

The guard sitting in the chamber looked at the two women. "No talking," he said.

"But mother..." Kylin started to say.

The guard jumped to his feet and held his sword over their heads. "I said no talking."

Kylin buried her head into her mother's chest and Laila held her protectively.

"She's done nothing," Laila said. "Why do you threaten us?"

"Milord said there's to be no talking," the guard yelled. "I should've tied you separate. Be glad I've allowed you to stay untied."

Kylin cried softly and the guard returned to the chair watching them.

"Mother..." Kylin said softly into her mother's chest.

Laila closed her eyes and held Kylin closer, stroking her hair. "Shhh. Have faith, Kylin."

The guard looked at the two and lifted his sword but was interrupted by footsteps on the stairs.

"I still say we should move them," Cadda said as he entered the room.

Claec laughed. "Where? What could be safer than the keep and the master's own chambers?" He walked over to the women and placed his hand gently on Kylin's cheek. "I'll have my prize soon enough."

Laila slapped Claec's hand away from Kylin. Claec's eyes narrowed and he slapped her face. "Even you will not keep me from my treasure."

Laila recoiled in pain, her cheek starting to display the imprint of Claec's hand.

"I'm only saying that Aethelhard is tricky. You don't know him the way I do," Cadda said.

Claec walked to the small window and laughed again. "Aethelhard could be dead along with Hutton for all we know. I gave orders that who ever killed them would be rewarded handsomely."

Kylin gasped, her fingers clutching at her mother's dress. Claec turned to face the two women, as he sneered. "Yes, you could be beholden to me if my plan works. Then what will you do? Your two protectors are gone." He snapped his fingers. "Their blood spilled on the cold ground where their souls will stay."

Kylin looked at him, her eyes wet with tears. She quickly buried her head back into her mother's chest, fresh tears spilling over her cheeks at the thought of her father and Aethelhard dead.

Laila looked to Claec; her eyes filled with hatred. "Haven't you done enough? Why must you continue to torture her?"

Claec laughed walking toward the door. "I'm only preparing her for things to come." He winked disappearing into the hall, his laughter echoing in the emptiness.

Cadda looked at them, then turned to the guard. "Make sure they don't escape. It'll be your head if they do."

"Yes, milord."

"Cadda!" Claec shouted from the stairs.

"I'm coming," Cadda shot back walking out of the room.

They continued down the tunnel, the air becoming pungent with the strong smell of incense. Aethelhard noticed the torch starting to flicker in a slow breeze filling the tunnel.

"The end of the tunnel must be ahead," Aethelhard said.

"What's that smell? It smells familiar," Reese said.

"Incense, I think," Aethelhard replied.

At the end of the tunnel was what appeared to be the remnants of a ladder that must have been used to access the tunnel. Now all that remained was a pile of rotted wood. Aethelhard looked up and saw that what ever was covering the tunnel was not very high. Reese clasped his hands and Aethelhard stepped into them, digging his feet into the narrow dirt walls to move up a little higher. He reached up and felt planks covering the tunnel like a floor had been laid over it. Gently he knocked on the wood, then slid back down to the tunnel below.

"It's covered with wood. Feels like wood planks. Might be a floor." Aethelhard brushed the loose dirt from his clothes.

"You think it's a cover or a floor?" Reese looked up at the wooden planks.

"Not sure. I didn't want to move it since I don't know where it would put us."

There was a noise on the ground above them. Someone was walking across the floor. The footsteps were soft. They stopped by the entrance of the tunnel where the boards covered it. Aethelhard's heart pounded. It was dark and if he was right about the planks, the torch could be filtering through it. He handed the torch to one of the knights and whispered. "Take this down the tunnel so the light can't be seen." The knight took the torch and walked back into the tunnel. Aethelhard looked up at the planks and waited.

The planks groaned. There was a soft knock on the wood. Aethelhard looked to Reese for a moment. Someone heard them. Aethelhard heard a voice but it was too far away to hear what he said. Reese clasped his hands again and Aethelhard climbed up the tunnel. He listened for several minutes not hearing a sound. His feet were cramping from having them dug into the dirt walls. He was just about to drop down when he heard the voice again. "Who's there?"

The voice was soft and Aethelhard strained to see if he recognized it.

There was soft knocking on the floor then the voice again. "Is someone there?"

Aethelhard took a chance and knocked lightly on the floor. The knock was answered on the other side. "Where are we?" Aethelhard said softly.

"The chapel."

Aethelhard nodded to Reese. That would explain the strong smell. It was incense. "Who are you?"

"I'm the priest. Who are you?"

"Aethelhard," he said softly. Reese just about dropped him when he said his name.

Reese couldn't believe Aethelhard told the stranger his name. "How do you know that's the priest? He may not be alone. It could be a trap."

Footsteps moved across the floor fading. Reese cursed. "Get your weapons ready and prepare for an attack."

It was quiet. Then faint footsteps were heard crossing the floor growing louder as they got closer to the tunnel entrance. Scraping was heard over the wood and Aethelhard jumped down preparing for an attack as well. The cover was turned; loose dirt fell into the tunnel as the cover was finally lifted from its resting spot.

The priest considered the tunnel and whispered. "Let me get you a stool." There was movement and then a stool was slowly lowered into the tunnel. "Be quick," the priest said. Aethelhard quickly climbed on the stool as the priest kept a watchful eye toward the door. "How many are there?"

"About fifteen of us," Aethelhard motioned for Reese to get on the stool with him.

"I can only safely hide two," the priest said.

Aethelhard crouched down with Reese. "He can only hide us. Tell the others to take the torch and go back to the cave. If we aren't back by the next night, they are to ride back to Elwyn Castle."

The priest kept his eyes on the door, looking out the windows now and then. "Hurry, there's not much time."

Reese jumped off the stool and spoke to the men still in the tunnel. "Go back to the cave but keep yourself hidden. Always keep at least one person awake to hear if anyone is coming there. We'll rejoin you as soon as possible. If we are not back by the next eve, you are to leave the cave and ride back to Elwyn." Reese hoisted himself back up with Aethelhard. The priest quickly placed the cover back over the tunnel, secured it and put the rug over it. He walked behind the holy table and pushed it over the rug and wooden cover. He motioned them to follow him to a small room. Inside was a small table and a bed. It was the priest's private room. He moved the bed, then pulled on a rope handle that was connected to a door on the floor. The door opened, and three steps led down to a cramped room. The priest took a lit candle from the small table and motioned the men to go down the stairs. He followed and pulled the door shut behind him.

"You are safe here," the priest said. "How did you find the tunnel? I thought I was the only one who knew of its existence."

"We found it by accident in the forest. I noticed the dirt around the boulder was moving away," Aethelhard sat on the dirt floor in the small room. "How did you know about it?"

"It's a secret tunnel built to protect the cross in case of attack."

Aethelhard looked at the priest furrowing his brows. "A cross?"

The priest continued. "It belongs to Milady D'arcy. It has been handed down through her family for generations. I was instructed to get it out of the castle if the castle ever fell under attack."

"Why's it still here?" Aethelhard said.

The priest smiled. "Who said it was?"

"Why are you talking about a cross?" Reese finally said. "We're here to rescue Milady Laila and Milady Kylin."

"Is Milord Hutton with you?" The priest asked.

"No, he was injured in the battle at Elwyn castle," Aethelhard said.

"Then you were successful and have retaken ownership of the castle?"

"Yes, what's left of it. It came with the cost of many men," Aethelhard said. "Who has taken over Nottes Castle?"

"The few men left to guard the castle were given mead with a potion in it. While they slept, Cadda and Claec took Milady Laila and Kylin captive. The men when they awoke were powerless. If they attacked the keep, Cadda and Claec would kill Milady Laila and Milady Kylin. More of Claec's men arrived this morning and secured the castle grounds. That's why you're not safe here. They already killed the rest of Milord Hutton's men. The servants were ordered to leave by this eve or be killed. I'm the only one left."

Aethelhard moved his feet over the dirt floor as he thought. "Do you know where they are keeping Laila and Kylin?"

"The only light I see is in Milord Hutton and Milady Laila's chambers. I would say that is the most likely place they are keeping them."

Aethelhard lifted his head, his eyes distant, as he tried to remember the layout of the castle grounds. "The chapel is close to the keep."

The priest nodded. "Yes, milord."

"Could you get us to the alcove at the side of the keep?"

The priest looked to Aethelhard curiously. "It's well hidden. I should be able to get you there safely."

"How's that going to get us in the keep?" Reese looked at the two curiously.

"If the priest can get us to the alcove, I can get us inside," Aethelhard said.

"It's too early to try now," the priest said as he climbed the stairs. "Once it's safe, I'll return for you." The priest quietly closed the door.

Aethelhard stretched out his legs and leaned against the dirt wall. "Might as well get some sleep. It may be another long night."

A few hours later Reese nudged Aethelhard awake. "I think it's time."

Aethelhard opened his sleepy eyes and sat up. It felt like he'd only slept minutes although he knew it was longer. "Has the priest come back yet?"

"No but I've heard him walking around. He must be getting something ready."

The bed scraped over the floor and the door creaked open. The priest walked down the stairs with dark heavy blankets. "Put these over you. They will keep the light from shining on your armor."

Aethelhard pulled the heavy blanket over him and waited for Reese to do the same.

"Not a word can be spoken by anyone," the priest said. "The men are watching for you. They know you are not at Elwyn castle and weren't a casualty." The men nodded, and the priest started up the stairs.

The night was still. Not even a breeze was felt as the men walked out of the chapel. The priest's footsteps were precise and quick as he led the men across the short path of dirt that led to the keep. The priest keeping them hidden in the shadows that danced over the sleepy land as they approached the alcove. Reaching the shadows, the priest left them and went back to the chapel.

Aethelhard walked the few feet from the alcove to the keep's walls and ran his fingers over the cold gray stones that formed the outer wall of the great tower. He cursed under his breath. What he was looking for seemed to elude him. He felt a hand on his shoulder, his body tensed as he searched under the blanket for his sword. Reese pointed toward the moon rising over the horizon. Its soft silvery light illuminating the land and creeping over the walls of the keep. Aethelhard had almost stepped from the shadows and into the moonlight unaware of what he was doing. His body moved from the light and sunk into the shadows that threatened to disappear as the moon started its ascent into the heavens.

Aethelhard leaned against the wall and closed his eyes. He had to find it. It was their only way into the keep to rescue Laila and Kylin. A warmth started to fall over him as light slowly filled the dark corners of his mind. There was a flash of light, a calm voice, and for only a moment he saw clearly what he was searching for. He quickly opened his eyes scanning the stones of the keep finally pausing on a spot just behind them. His fingers moved over the stones then sunk deeply into the opening. He found the groove in the stones and pulled slowly. The stones swung open revealing the passageway. He motioned to Reese. The two men melted into the shadows of the passageway as the stones moved back into place.

Inside the passageway, they kept their blankets on so that any light filtering through the stones wouldn't pick up the glint from their armor. He looked toward the loose dirt path which led to the stairs and motioned for Reese to follow him.

They walked slowly not making a sound. The stone stairs carried them higher in the keep. Aethelhard stopped suddenly hearing a muffled sound. He continued up the stairs, the sound growing louder as they approached the bed chambers. Aethelhard now recognized the sound as snoring. The guard must be asleep. He tried to peer into the room through the cracks in the stone. Not even a candle was lit in the chambers and darkness abounded.

Aethelhard started pushing on the stones. There was a soft click and the wall moved slowly, scraping the stone floor. He stopped after hearing the groan of a chair and movement in the room. He tried to look through the darkness but all he saw were shadows. He looked to Reese and they waited. In a few moments, the sound of snoring was heard once more. Aethelhard started to slowly push on the stones again. The heavy stones groaning softly as they moved.

Reese placed his hand on Aethelhard's shoulder bringing his fingers to his lips in a sign of quiet just as the stones were about to swing open into the room. Aethelhard paused, listening. Not hearing anything, he pushed again on the stones but stopped. This time he did hear something. His heartbeat wildly in his chest. Beads of sweat forming on his brow and down his back. He raised a brow hearing a familiar knocking on the stone. It was the same pattern he heard the priest use on the wooden cap of the tunnel. But how did the priest get into the room unless…it was a trap. He motioned for Reese to pull his sword as his fingers wrapped around his own sword. He pushed on the wall of stones and they opened into the darkened room.

A single shard of moonlight pierced the small window of the chambers. Aethelhard froze seeing someone move in the room. He raised his sword, the glint of the sharp blade giving the only hint he was there. He felt a hand on his right wrist and flinched, moving his sword toward the right. With only inches until the blade of the sword would impact on its intended target, he caught a glimpse of her face. It was Laila. He tried to stop the sword from hitting her, but the movement was already in motion after many years of practice. He did the only thing he could; he dropped the sword. The guard awoke amid the clattering of the sword as it hit the stone floor.

"Who's there?" The guard shouted.

Aethelhard quickly picked up his sword then ran to the bed picking up Kylin. In her sleepy state she beat on him.

"Let me go!"

The clashing of swords filled the room. Aethelhard grabbed Kylin's arms to keep her from thrashing and falling from his shoulder.

"Kylin, it's me," he finally said breaking the silence.

She stopped thrashing and looked at him. "How did you get here?"

"That doesn't matter." Aethelhard heard shouts from the outside as the other men ran toward the keep. The clashing of swords stopped as a groan followed a gurgling sound. Aethelhard ran back to the passageway with someone right behind him. The stone wall quickly closing.

Breathing heavily, Reese whispered, "We have to get out of here."

Laila started down the stairs as the Claec's men reached the room.

Cadda looked down at the dead man, anger quickly covering his face. "Capture them. I don't care if they're dead or alive except for Aethelhard. I want him alive. I'll drive the blade through his heart to end his miserable life."

"We can't leave outside the keep," Aethelhard said. "They'll have it surrounded."

"Shh," Laila said continuing her descent down the stairs. They reached the foot of the stairs and Laila stopped, waiting for Reese to step into the soft dirt. She pointed to the last stone of the stairs. "Get on either side of the step and pull."

Aethelhard heard the pounding on the wall in the chambers. They must have found something to try to break the stones apart. There wasn't much time. He put Kylin down and reached to the step with Reese on the other side. They both groaned as they tried to pull the step away, the pounding from upstairs growing louder.

"Hurry," Laila said looking anxiously to the top of the stairs. "They're going to break through the wall any time."

Finally, the step started to move. Aethelhard and Reese pulled on it with all their strength and the step moved away. Laila pushed Kylin through the small opening. "Crawl on your stomach." Kylin started crawling through the small opening. Laila was right behind her pushing her through. Reese and Aethelhard squeezed through the small opening just as the crash of stones filled the stairway. Footsteps were coming down the stairs with Cadda yelling in the background. Aethelhard pulled the rope that was attached to the step to move it back in place.

"Quickly, this way," Laila said.

He turned following the others down the narrow dirt passageway jumping into a narrow tunnel. They ran until they came to the end of the tunnel, but Laila didn't stop. She lowered her shoulder toward the dirt wall and burst through it.

"You made it," a voice said.

"Yes, although they are looking for us," Laila said.

"It's what I thought with all the commotion," he answered.

"Did you get it?" Laila started running down the tunnel.

"Yes," the voice answered.

Aethelhard had time to get a brief look. The dirt wall was only a separation between the tunnel under the chapel and the one they followed out of the keep. He heard voices above him in the chapel and ran to catch up with the others.

"Get the horses ready," Laila said scrambling from the tunnel past the boulder. "Move the boulder over the tunnel. It will stop them if they find the tunnel in the chapel." Reese and the Priest pushed on the boulder and it came crashing over the tunnel entrance.

They heard the drawbridge being lowered as men started to leave the castle grounds. Aethelhard grabbed Kylin placing her on the back of his horse. "Hold tight," he shouted. "It may be a rough ride." He looked to Reese and saw he had Laila on his horse.

"Are you sure you'll be all right," Laila said to the Priest. The horse reared, and Laila grabbed hold of Reese.

"Yes, milady. Now run, like the wind." The Priest slapped the horse's rump and ran toward the forest. Reese's horse reared once more then started galloping down the stream. Aethelhard caught up to them, the other knights behind them.

"Do you remember where we are?" Laila shouted above the splashing water.

Aethelhard looked around and recognized the road ahead as the road he had seen Laila on with the wagon. "Yes."

"Take a left on the road, then a right on the path by the well that leads into the forest," Laila shouted. "We'll follow."

Aethelhard dug his heels into the horse's sides. Soon, they were following the narrow path through the forest. Just as the sun was about to rise over the horizon, they emerged from the forest. Elwyn Castle was in view.

"How's the wall coming?" Hutton stepped into the early morning sun looking over the burned wall. He knew they were in danger until repairs to the wall were made.

"We're further along than we expected," the knight said. "Now that the battle from Scotland has ended for now, the King allowed his men to return to their own lands."

Hutton walked toward the wall. He had a feeling it was only a brief break in the battle but perhaps it would be enough to get the repairs completed. "Has anyone seen the King?"

"No, milord."

Hutton turned his head toward the tower after hearing a trumpet announcing someone arriving. "Who's coming?" Hutton shouted.

"Milady and your daughter," the man shouted back.

Hutton felt his heart leap from his chest. "Are you sure?"

"Yes, milord."

Hutton ran to the drawbridge as it was being lowered. Even though everyone was covered with mud and leaves, it was the most beautiful sight he'd ever seen. He walked over to Laila and wrapped his arms around her as she slid off the horse. "Laila, I was afraid I'd never see you alive," he said softly into her hair.

Laila laid her tired head on Hutton's chest, her arms wrapping around him. "Nor did I for a while. It's because of Aethelhard and Reese, that Kylin and I are reunited with you."

"Is the castle still standing?" Hutton said softly, stroking her hair.

"For now. But it's difficult to say if it will for long. Cadda and Claec are ruthless. They'll stop at nothing until they find it," Laila said softly.

"Did they?"

"It's hidden for now."

Hutton nodded. "Good. Go rest, my dear."

Hutton walked over to Aethelhard and Reese. "I am indebted to you both for risking your lives and rescuing my wife and daughter."

Aethelhard shook the loose dirt from his boots. "I'm sorry we couldn't take the castle back. There weren't enough men."

"But you brought back my wife and daughter," Hutton said. "Castles can be rebuilt, flesh and blood can not." Hutton continued to walk with Aethelhard toward the castle leaving the others to tend to the horses. "I also owe you an apology for my previous actions against you."

"Accepted," Aethelhard said. He wanted to talk more with Hutton but that would have to wait. After two battles and two days of very little sleep, his mind was a jumble. "If you'll excuse me, I'll be going to my chambers."

Hutton smiled. "Of course. We can talk after you've rested. The Scotland battle has ended…for now."

Aethelhard snapped his head toward Hutton. "It has?"

Hutton nodded. "We'll talk later."

Aethelhard looked over the grounds. He saw more men than what he remembered tending to the damage the castle had sustained during the battle. All the dead that once covered the grounds were buried as well.

"And the King?" Aethelhard asked.

Hutton shook his head. "He's alive but I haven't heard anymore."

Aethelhard placed his hand on the familiar handle of the door that led into the castle. "We'll talk later." Hutton was walking back to the damaged castle wall. Aethelhard walked into his chamber for some much-needed rest.

Aethelhard woke to the smell of fresh bread and roasting meat. He also heard the men shouting and stones being moved as the men worked to repair the wall. It didn't take Hutton long to get a castle back in order.

He walked into the afternoon sun. Hutton was directing the men on the stone placement.

Hutton turned hearing someone approaching. "Feeling better?"

Aethelhard stretched as he looked over the partially repaired wall. "Hungry but better."

"Dinner should be ready from the smell of bread and meat." Hutton turned and started for the main hall. "The wall should be repaired soon as well."

Aethelhard followed him. "We'll need to go back and take Nottes Castle as soon as this one is repaired."

"Yes, I've been thinking of that," Hutton said entering the main hall.

"Will Laila and Kylin be joining us?"

"No," said Hutton. "I've already arranged to have food brought to their chambers."

The two men sat down and started to eat. About halfway through, there was a knock on the door.

"Milord, there is someone here to see you," the squire said to Hutton.

Hutton looked at the squire then took another bite of the roasted meat. "Can't he wait?"

"He's the King's messenger."

"Is the King with him?" Aethelhard questioned taking a gulp of mead.

"No, it's only the messenger," the squire said.

"Then bring him in," Hutton said.

The squire nodded to the door and the messenger stepped inside. He bowed before them.

"Milord Hutton, I have a message from the King."

"Yes, what is it?" Hutton said quickly.

"In reward for your service to His Royal Majesty, Castle Nottes has been taken back and will soon be ready for your arrival."

"What?" Hutton stood, his chair crashing behind him. "Where are Cadda and Claec?"

The messenger placed a bag on the floor then a small leather bag on the table. "A gift from His Royal Majesty for your service as well. The bag on the table is for Milord Elwyn."

Hutton looked curiously at the messenger, then walked over to the bag and opened it. He closed it without saying a word about what was inside. "Thank His Royal Majesty for me."

Aethelhard opened the bag on the table. Shaking it three sapphires fell into his hand. Aethelhard placed them back into the bag. "Thank His Royal Majesty

The messenger bowed then left the room.

Aethelhard looked at the bag on the floor curiosity getting the better of him. "What's in the bag?"

Hutton looked to the bag then at a servant who was standing nearby. "Take the bag to the dogs."

Aethelhard watched as the servant picked up the bag. The dogs followed him out of the room jumping toward the bag.

"Do you think it's wise to give the King's gift to the dogs?" Aethelhard finally said.

Hutton smiled as he heard the dogs start to fight outside. "I have no need for it."

Aethelhard leaned toward him and took another bite of the roasted venison. "What is it?"

"Cadda's head," Hutton said.

Aethelhard almost choked on his meat. "Cadda's head?"

"Yes," Hutton took another bite of the roasted meat. "We'll be leaving tomorrow for Nottes Castle. I have business of my own to attend to."

After finishing their supper, they both were quiet staring into the fireplace. The dogs had stopped fighting over their "supper" and only a growl was heard now and then.

"I've a long day tomorrow, said Hutton as he finished his mead. "I think I'll take an early retire."

Aethelhard nodded. "I should get some rest too. It's been a long few days."

Even as Aethelhard tried to sleep, he kept tossing and turning through the night. In the early morning, he finally gave up and dressed. He picked up a biscuit and walked outside. There was still a chill in the early morning air as Aethelhard walked outside. One of the knights walked toward him.

"Did you wish to see me, milord?"

"Yes," Aethelhard said walking toward the stables. "Is everything ready for Hutton and Laila's departure?"

"Yes," the knight said. "They should be departing soon."

Aethelhard looked over the stables and saw preparations were well under way. "I've decided to join them on their journey back to Nottes Castle. You think you can run the castle until my return?"

The knight looked at him both surprised and happy. "Yes, milord. It would be an honor."

"Fine," Aethelhard watched as Hutton approach the stable.

"Good for you to see us off," Hutton said. "It's a full day's journey back to the castle."

"I've decided to go back with you," Aethelhard said bringing his own steed from the stable.

Hutton smiled and Aethelhard saw a glint in his eyes. "I thought there was more than enough work to keep you busy here."

"There is," Aethelhard replied. "I'm leaving the castle in good hands until my return."

Aethelhard mounted his steed, then reached down to helped Kylin sit in front of him. He brought the reins around her. He looked back to see if everyone was ready. Some of the men had already started out of the castle. Aethelhard lightly moved his heels into the steed's sides. The steed started toward the others at a trot. Laila smiled to Hutton.

They journeyed through the day. As the sun set, they rode through the village leading to Nottes Castle. Many of the villagers came out of their cottages when they heard the lord and lady were back. They waved to them as they rode through the village.

"Your father is well liked," Aethelhard said as they left the village headed toward the castle.

"Yes," said Kylin. "Father has always been a fair man."

Aethelhard looked toward the castle grounds after hearing the clanking of the drawbridge coming down. It was good to see things returning to normal. The horses' feet clopped over the drawbridge as they rode across. The great drawbridge being brought back up after the last horse crossed.

Aethelhard looked around as he led his steed to the stables. It looked as though the damage had been minimal from the scrimmage that was fought earlier. The great wall around the castle was intact. There were only two buildings that had been damaged. He marveled how the King's men were able to take back the castle in such an efficient manner. He pulled on the reins bringing the steed to a stop as they neared the stable building. He brought the reins over Kylin then dismounted his horse. After handing the reins to a stable boy, he reached placing his hands around Kylin's waist and helped her down. Kylin smiled to him. He smiled back, still not understanding why he had become so protective of her. He'd felt that way since they left Elwyn Castle to rescue her. The thought of her at another man's hands still started that churning in his stomach.

"There's a light supper, milord," the servant said as Hutton dismounted his horse.

"Good," Hutton helped Laila from her horse. "Make sure there is plenty of mead. The trip here has made me thirsty."

"Yes, milord," the servant said and quickly disappeared into kitchen.

Kylin and Aethelhard followed Hutton and Laila into the large hall. A light supper of bread, fruit, and soup was soon brought out. They were silent through supper after the tiring journey.

"May I be excused," Kylin said as she finished the last of her mead.

Hutton looked a little concerned. "Are you feeling all right?"

"Yes, father," she replied. "Just a little tired from the journey here."

Hutton nodded and Kylin left the room.

"I believe I should be going as well," Laila said. "I would like to check the kitchen and a few other things to make sure everything is ready for tomorrow."

Aethelhard moved toward the hearth. He finished his mead setting the mug on a small table. "I think I'll retire as well."

"Going to your chamber so soon?" Hutton's eyes never leaving the hearth.

"Shortly. I thought I'd take a walk in the gardens first to clear my mind of the recent events." Aethelhard walked outside and toward the path that lead to the garden.

The air was already cool, and a light breeze rustled through the leaves of the trees. He sat on a bench, absently picking a rose from the bush. As he looked at the rose, he thought of the time he'd found Kylin in the garden crying. She too, had picked a rose and mentioned that even the rose knew of her sadness. It wasn't sadness that brought him to the garden tonight but something else. A feeling he'd not felt before. So much had happened in the last few days. He set the rose on the bench and started to walk down the path.

His footsteps taking him to the more secluded part of the garden. He turned looking once more at the bench where he'd seen Kylin crying that night so long ago, but the bench was empty. Only the moonlight played over it tonight. As he walked closer, something on the bench caught his eye. He reached down and picked up a rose. He raised a brow as he felt the dampness on the rose's petals.

"It was good you could join us for our journey home," a voice nearby spoke.

Aethelhard jumped not expecting to find anyone in the garden this late. He turned as Kylin stepped from the shadows.

"I wanted to make sure you made it home," Aethelhard said.

"Would you care to join me for a walk?"

Aethelhard bowed to Kylin. "I'd be honored to join the most beautiful flower of the garden for an evening walk."

Kylin laughed softly and started walking down the path with Aethelhard beside her. "It's been a rather eventful few days since our last walk here."

"Yes, it has," Aethelhard replied. "More so than I'd expected but it's been worth it."

"Why is that?"

Aethelhard looked a little surprised. "Your father and I have managed to regain possession of our castles again."

"Oh," Kylin said softly.

They walked in silence. Was she so naïve that she didn't understand the dangers they'd gone through to regain their respective castles? Certainly, she must have for even she was held captive for a while. He thought again of Claec having his hands on her, his hands forming fists beside him as they walked.

"Why are you angry?"

Aethelhard looked to her quickly. "What are you talking about?

Kylin pointed. "Your hands have formed fists. Why?"

He looked down to his hands quickly releasing his fingers. "It was nothing."

Kylin canted her head, then looked to the willow tree. "Do you remember the first time we were under the willow tree?"

How could he not? She'd almost gotten him thrown out of the castle after that little antic of hers. Not to mention almost killed. He paused in front of the willow and watched as she stepped off the path. Her lithe form outlined in the moonlight until she disappeared behind the curtain of green. "Kylin, I'm not going back there." He waited for her return. "I mean it Kylin. You almost got me killed the last time." Still not a sound came from under the willow. Taking a deep resigned breath, he walked toward the willow. That woman was going to get him killed yet. His fingers parted the curtain of green and he walked through.

Kylin was sitting on the ground, the branches of the willow forming a dome over them. She looked up and smiled to him. Aethelhard sat beside her.

"I knew you'd come."

"I wouldn't be so sure of myself, milady."

"But you came."

He pulled her to face him. "Why are you trying to get me killed?"

Kylin blinked, turning her head away from him.

He closed his eyes, then reached over, gently cupping her chin with his fingers. He brought her eyes back to him. "I'm sorry. I shouldn't have accused you of that."

Kylin pulled away from him. "Why do you think I want you dead?"

He moved closer to her. "I don't know. After our last meeting here and then having to rescue you, I've become a little tentative."

"I didn't ask you to rescue me," she said softly.

"How could I not? I couldn't let Claec have his way with you."

"You may already be too late. He could have already damaged me."

Aethelhard grabbed her shoulders pulling her to him his eyes desperately searching her eyes. "Did he?"

She pulled away. "What difference would it make? I only want to kill you, or have you forgotten so soon." He saw the hurt in her eyes.

"Kylin, that is not what I meant, and you know it," he said as his own words were thrown back at him and burned a hole to his soul.

"Then what do you mean?" She pulled away from him, turning her back toward him.

Aethelhard grabbed hold of her turning her so she was facing him, his hands tightly holding her shoulders. "This." He reached down and kissed her softly. Gradually letting go of her shoulders, he wrapped his arms around her, feeling her body relax and starting to press against him. He broke the kiss and looked into her eyes.

She smiled, her fingers moving slowly down his arms. "We should come to the willow tree more often," she finally said.

Aethelhard took hold of her hand. He led her out from under the tree and back to the path. "No, we shouldn't."

"Why?" She spoke innocently.

He looked at her as the moonlight washed over her delicate features, then quickly turned away. "Because every time we do, I seem to get into trouble." He released her hand as they stepped back onto the worn path.

She laughed as they walked, her hand slipping back into his hand.

Kylin reached up to softly kiss his cheek as they exited the garden. "Thank you for accompanying me on my walk."

Aethelhard's eyes closed a moment, her lips softly pressed to his cheek. He released her hand and bowed. "It was my pleasure."

She smiled then walked toward the keep.

Aethelhard watched her, wondering why he felt a fluttering in his stomach. He couldn't be in love with her. She'd been nothing but trouble since he got here. But he couldn't shake the way he felt. He walked to the hall, running his fingers roughly through his hair.

"Have a nice walk?"

He turned and saw Hutton sitting on a bench next to the door of the hall. "It's a nice eve for a walk," Aethelhard sat down.

Hutton poured a glass of mead and handed it to him. "Thought you might like some mead after your walk."

Aethelhard took the mug and drank half of the mead.

"Must have been a long walk," Hutton refilled Aethelhard's mug.

"It was," Aethelhard took another long drink of mead.

"I should start looking for another suitor for Kylin."

"Do you think it's wise after all she's gone through recently?"

Hutton laughed. "She looked fine when she came from the garden tonight." He looked at Aethelhard and smiled.

"Uh…yes, an evening walk is always good," he stuttered.

"I'll be a lot more careful in looking for her suitor this time. He'll have to be a man of outstanding background, courage, and someone I can trust with my little girl."

Aethelhard took another gulp of the mead, trying hard not to look at him. "You have anyone in mind?"

"A couple…one in particular."

"That's good," Aethelhard refilled his mug. "She'll need someone to protect her."

Aethelhard thought of their kiss under the willow tree. He felt his stomach fluttering just as it had in the garden. Quickly he gulped his mead and tried to forget their kiss. It would be good for Kylin to have a husband who could control her. Obviously, it wasn't him. It was just like when they were younger and playing together. She always got him in trouble. There are some things even time doesn't change he thought shaking his head.

Hutton interrupted his thoughts. "It's good to be back home."

Chapter 7

"Have you seen, milord?" The squire had been looking most of the morning for Hutton to deliver an important message.

The young girl looked up from the mending and shook her head. "I've not seen milord today. Check with the steward. He usually knows where milord can be found."

The squire walked to the steward sitting on a bench outside. "Have you seen milord today?"

The steward was looking over more papers. "Of course, I've seen him. He's in the room off the main hall." He quickly looked at the squire. "Don't bother him." The squire started for the hall and the steward quickly ran after him. "He's much work to do."

The squire knocked on the door.

Hutton looked up from the piles of papers he'd been working on. "Yes?"

The squire entered. "Milord Aethelhard would like to speak to you about an important matter as soon as possible."

Hutton pushed the piles of papers away. "Did he say what the matter was about?"

"No, milord, only that it was important."

"Find Aethelhard and tell him I'll meet with him in my chambers."

The squire bowed. "Yes, milord."

The steward called after him about important matters that needed tending but Hutton continued walking, ignoring him. If this is what he thought it was about, it was a much more important matter.

Hutton paced in front of the hearth. He thought he knew why Aethelhard wanted to see him, but the possibility of surprises always kept him unnerved. He looked out the window and over his land. Everything was back to normal although the disappearance of Claec kept him cautious. A knock on the door interrupted his thoughts. "Enter," he said.

"Good eve, Hutton," Aethelhard said as he walked in.

"Ah, it's good to see you. It's been a while since we've talked. What's on your mind?" Hutton poured some mead into a mug and handed it to him. "All is going well, I hope."

Aethelhard took a long drink of the mead. "Yes, everything has been going well…almost too well," he chuckled. His face suddenly turned serious and he drained the mead. "I've come to ask something of you and Milady Laila."

Hutton's brow furrowed after hearing their titles. It was something serious indeed. "Yes," he said calmly.

"Have you found a suitor for Kylin yet?"

"No," he said watching Aethelhard.

"I know this is rather unconventional and I'd understand if your answer is no especially if you have someone else in mind."

"How can I answer when I've not heard the question."

"I wish to ask for your daughter's hand in marriage," Aethelhard finally said.

Hutton smiled and put his hand on Aethelhard's shoulder. "You've proven your courage and protected Kylin better than any man I've met. It would be an honor to call you son. I'm sure Laila will agree."

He refilled the mugs. "Have you spoken to Kylin about this?"

"No. I thought it proper to ask you and Milady Laila first."

"I wish you the best of luck with her." Hutton chuckled. "You know her best from childhood. She can be difficult at times. You have the best chance of winning her heart or what ever she's heard from the troubadours in the village."

"This love she speaks of is still rather new to me as well." Aethelhard shook his head. "I'll do everything I can to make her happy all the same."

Hutton smiled. I'm sure you will. "You've been gone for a while from your own castle. You must want to get back soon."

"Yes, I've been gone longer than I anticipated. I'll leave Elwyn Castle for Nottes Castle as soon as I can for the wedding." Aethelhard paused then looked toward the garden. "I'll ask her tonight to be my bride. With luck, she'll consent."

As soon as Aethelhard opened the door to leave the steward rushed inside. "Milord, have you looked over the papers yet?"

Aethelhard walked down the hall then smiled hearing Hutton's muffled voice as the steward tried to talk to him. Obviously Kylin wasn't his only problem.

It was getting late in the evening as Aethelhard walked the grounds trying to find Kylin. He'd not seen her since supper. He looked toward the garden. She must be there, probably under the willow tree again. This time, however, would be different from the others, he thought walking toward the garden path. He approached the willow tree quietly, his back against the foliage. Quickly he parted the overhanging willow thinking he'd surprised her. Kylin sat with her back toward the trunk of the tree. She looked up and smiled.

"It's about time." Her eyes twinkling as she looked to capture his eyes. He reached down for her hands and pulled her toward him. "You know, if we keep meeting like this, father will wonder what we are doing…" Her words trailing as his hands lightly touched the sides of her cheeks kissing her deeply. Her body relaxed against him, her arms slowly moving under his arms, then up his strong back. She took a deep breath at last realizing how strong he'd become over the years. As their kiss ended, their eyes staying locked, a gentle smile spread over her lips. His hands moved slowly over her shoulders curious what her answer would be. A bead of sweat touched his forehead and started slowly sliding to the edge of his brow.

Kylin cocked her head. With a gentle, soft hand she brushed it away. "Are you feeling ill?"

"No." He turned his eyes away for a moment, suddenly feeling a need for her. He captured her eyes once more, his hands slowly caressing her arms, then lightly grasping her hands. "There's something I must ask you."

"Of course,"

"I still don't know of this love you speak of, but I would like to learn more about it with you." He felt her hands tremble. Hopefully she would say yes. He had to forge ahead. It was too late to turn back now. "Kylin, will you marry me?"

"Are you asking me to marry you?" She wanted to make sure she heard the words correctly and wasn't dreaming.

"Yes." Aethelhard brought her hand to his lips and kissed it softly.

"Yes." Tears spilled from her eyes, slowly wetting her cheeks. She didn't know if Aethelhard had talked with her father, but she would convince him to agree with the engagement no matter how long it took.

They walked hand in hand down the garden path toward the castle. As soon as they reached outside the path, Aethelhard let go of her hand.

"Not backing out already, are you?" Kylin studied his dark green eyes.

"Of course not but the marriage hasn't been announced. We must keep some propriety." He opened the door to the keep for her to enter.

"But it will be announced very soon."

They walked down the hall to her chambers as her hand tried to brush against his. He moved his hand closer to his body to keep some space between them. He opened the door to her chambers surprising Kylin's attendant, Marie.

"Sleep well." He bowed slightly to her as she entered her chambers then closed the door behind her.

Marie looked at the brilliant glow to Kylin's face. "Did something happen tonight?"

"No, why do you ask?"

"I've known you since you were a babe. I've never seen your face glowing so brightly."

Kylin ran to Marie and hugged her. "Aethelhard has asked me to marry him."

Marie's eyes opened wide. "Does your father know of this?"

Kylin's eyes twinkled. "It doesn't matter. I will convince him one way or another."

"You would be the one to convince him," Marie said just before there was a light knock on the door.

Kylin raced to the door thinking it was Aethelhard. Instead it was her mother. "Mother, is something wrong?" She was hoping her father didn't send her mother to tell her she couldn't marry Aethelhard.

"That depends," she said as she walked into Kylin's chambers.

The glow was starting to leave Kylin's face. "On what?"

Laila smiled at her daughter. "Aethelhard spoke with your father earlier this evening."

Kylin ran to her mother's arms. "Did father give his blessing?"

Laila ran her hand over the back of Kylin's head. "Of course, dear. We both are so happy for you and Aethelhard."

"Has a date been set?" Kylin looked hopefully at her.

"Not yet, dear." Laila stroked Kylin's hair. "It may be a few weeks."

"Why?"

"Aethelhard must return to his castle. He's been gone a long time. Also, a notice must be put on the chapel door."

"How long will it be?" Her glow once again quickly fading.

"It will be soon. You should retire, my dear." Laila hugged her daughter again before closing the door.

Hutton heard the quiet steps of his wife on the cool stone floor. He watched as she opened the door. "Well?"

Laila smiled. "He asked her this evening. She has agreed to marry him."

Hutton sighed with relief. "Finally."

She took off her outer robe and climbed into the large bed under the warm animal skins. "She's quite excited. I think she'd marry him tomorrow if she could."

Hutton pulled Laila to him. "I'll discuss it with him tomorrow morning before he leaves for his castle then I'll put up the notice on the chapel door myself."

The next morning broke with a cloudless sky and a bright sun. "Aethelhard should make good time getting to his castle," Hutton thought as he walked to the chapel to hang the wedding notice.

The priest, hearing the nail going into the wooden door, opened it a crack to see who was there. "Milord D'arcy, what brings you out so early this morning?"

"Sorry to have bothered you, Father. I was putting up a wedding notice on the door."

"Oh? Who is getting married?" The priest opened the door to see the notice.

Hutton smiled. "Kylin, finally."

The priest was curious but kept his reactions to himself. "Who will she be marrying?"

"Aethelhard Elwyn."

The priest smiled and nodded. "It will be a good union for both. When do wish to have the wedding?"

"In about three weeks. Aethelhard needs to go to his castle for a few days. We'll have plenty of time to plan the wedding."

The priest bowed his head as he closed the door. "I look forward to the wedding and festivities."

After two long days of riding, Aethelhard arrived at his castle. From the village, everything looked secure and moving as usual. The market was operating, homes had been rebuilt, and livestock were roaming around the grassland. His steed clopped slowly across the draw bridge.

Reese ran from the stables with a stable boy closely following him. "Good evening, Aethelhard. It's good to see you again."

Aethelhard dismounted his steed handing the reins to the young boy. "It's good to see you again, Reese. It appears you have everything in order."

"It wasn't very difficult. Milord D'arcy did a lot before he handed everything over to me."

They walked toward the supper hall. "Then my stay will be shorter than I thought."

"Leaving so soon?"

"Yes. I need to return to Nottes castle as soon as I can." Aethelhard took off his outer coat as they entered the hall.

Reese gave him a confused look. "I thought Nottes castle was in order."

"It is." Aethelhard sat as the table and took a large bite of meat. "You'll be going back with me."

Reese raised a brow. "Oh?"

"We must return for a wedding."

"Whose wedding?" Reese sat down at the table.

Aethelhard looked up from the table and smiled at Reese. "Mine."

"Kylin?" Reese asked tentatively.

"Yes," Aethelhard smiled.

Reese slapped him on his back. "Congratulations. It will be good to have a Misses around the castle."

Aethelhard nodded and smiled. "Yes, it will." He took a long drink of his mead. "What matters do I need to attend to before I can leave for Nottes castle?"

All his official duties were completed except one…the ring. Aethelhard tapped his fingers on the worn table as he gazed absently into the flames of the hearth. He was just waiting on the goldsmith to finish Kylin's ring. The three sapphires the King gave him had come at a good time. The goldsmith was using them for a ring for Kylin. He wanted to check on the ring again but knew his presence would only hurry the goldsmith. He wanted the ring to be perfect. He decided it best to retire for the evening and check on the ring tomorrow.

Aethelhard arose in the early morning. He finished his hot mead and fresh bread before leaving to the goldsmith. He opened the door to the goldsmith's building and saw he was polishing the ring. The goldsmith turned to see him walk inside then went back to his polishing.

"The ring is almost finished, Milord. I just need to finish the polish."

Aethelhard looked over his shoulder and smiled. The sapphires sparkled just like Kylin's own blue eyes. "You've done well. I'll see to it that you are handsomely rewarded. I'm going to get ready for the trip to Nottes castle. Bring the ring when you are finished."

"Yes, milord."

Aethelhard was tightening the straps oh his stead when Reese approached him. "I saw the goldsmith. He asked that I bring this to you."

Aethelhard smiled as the silver and sapphire ring dropped in his hand.

"Is everything ready for the ride to Nottes castle?"

Reese mounted his horse. "The messenger left early last evening to let Milord D'arcy know of our arrival." He nodded to the other knights to mount their horses as well. "Already to go."

Aethelhard slipped the ring into a small drawstring pouch into his pocket attaching the strings to the small slit at the top of his pocket. He mounted his stead lightly digging his heels into its side to start the ride to Nottes.

Chapter 8

Kylin was trying hard not to miss Aethelhard but it seemed she was looking the direction he'd come every few minutes. "Marie, I don't think I can wait much longer."

Marie smiled as she looked over Kylin's wedding dress. "You must be patient. He'll be here soon."

Kylin sighed. "I know."

Marie shook the dress a little and held it up to Kylin. "Looks like the dress will fit you just fine. This was your mother's wedding dress. The new blue cloak and pearls on the sleeves add an elegant touch." She set the dress on Kylin's bed. "You should try it on so there's time to make any adjustments."

Kylin looked at the dreaded laced corset. "Let's just get this over with."

After corset was laced and the dress put on, Marie stepped back to admire it. "You look like a princess."

At the end of Marie's words there was a quiet knock at the door. "Kylin, are you here?"

Kylin turned to look at herself in the mirror. "Yes, mother." She moved the dress around and felt the velvety touch of her cloak with her long light brown hair tumbling down her back.

Laila opened the wooden door. "Kylin, it's beautiful. You do look like a princess." She winked to Marie as a sign that she heard her words.

Kylin shifted in the dress trying to move her shoulders and now her tiny waist. "Must I wear this corset?"

"Your waist is small, but the waist of the dress is for a corset. I know you don't like the constrictive corset but I've news of something you want to hear."

Kylin quickly turned toward Laila. "What is it mother?"

"Aethelhard will be returning in a few days."

Kylin threw her arm around her mother. "I've missed him so."

Laila smiled. "I know dear." She then turned to Marie. "There's much to do to get ready for the wedding." Laila smiled toward Kylin. "I'm sure they'll want to wed as soon as they can."

"Yes, mother, there is much to do." Kylin turned toward Marie. "First I must get out of this confining dress."

Laila laughed softly. "Be glad you don't wear one all of the time."

Kylin turned toward Laila just as Marie unlaced the corset. She took a deep unconfining breath.

Laila then joined Hutton on the grounds outside of the keep. "Is the dowry completed?"

Hutton was watching the knights set up an area for jousting and other entertainment. "That was completed and signed before Aethelhard left for his castle. The carpenter will have to make at least two or three tables for the feast."

Laila nodded then turned toward the kitchen. "I need to make sure everything is ready for the wedding feast. I'll also make sure Kylin's portrait is completed before Aethelhard arrives."

Laila arrived at the dining area and kitchen to see everyone working hard to prepare for the feast. As she was passing the breeze way, she found Thaddeus. "Thaddeus."

The painter bowed then waited for instructions.

"We would like to get a portrait of Kylin wearing her wedding dress. Perhaps tomorrow as the sun is coming over the horizon."

"Yes, milady."

Laila smiled. "I have the perfect spot in the garden in front of the willow tree."

"Yes, milady."

"I'll make sure Kylin is properly dressed and arrives before dawn."

Thaddeus bowed. "Yes, milady."

Laila walked toward the garden, then sat on a stone bench. The painter was the easy part of the portrait. Now…she had to make sure Kylin was there with her hair done and dressed at dawn. She sighed. Kylin never was an early riser. Laila decided not to tell Kylin. She'd awaken Kylin herself before dawn.

Kylin was restless through the night and had just gone to sleep when Laila knocked then opened the door to her chamber.

She gently shook Kylin. "Kylin, get up."

Kylin turned over in the bed to escape whoever was trying to awaken her.

Laila shook her again. "Kylin, you need to get up."

She barely opened her eyes then curled into a ball with the furs on her bed. "The sun isn't even up. Go away."

Laila shook her head then pulled the furs off her.

Kylin's eyes flew open to see her mother with her hands on her waist. "Kylin, you need to get up, now." Marie stood by the hearth letting Leila awaken her.

"Why do I have to get up before dawn? I've not even had a cup of mead."

"You can have your mead after your portrait is completed."

"Portrait? What portrait?"

Marie took off her night clothes as Laila checked her clothes for the portrait then handed the corset to Marie. "Your bridal portrait."

Kylin was now fully awake.

"Marie! Stop lacing the corset so tight." Marie looked to Laila.

"Go ahead, Marie." Laila turned toward Kylin. "The corset must be worn with the wedding dress." She was now combing Kylin's hair until it shined in the dim light of the fire in the hearth. "Kylin, I know you don't like any of this, but it must be done. Stop making this harder than it has to be."

Kylin looked at her mother, her pale blue eyes looking as if they were on fire. She finally sat on the overstuffed ottoman, her arms crossed, lips pouting, and just in a general bad mood.

After finally getting her dressed and ready for her portrait, Laila and Marie walked with Kylin to the garden. Marie was careful to make sure the hem of her wedding gown didn't get dirty.

"Why are we going to the garden?" Kylin was perplexed. Most portraits were painted inside the castle.

"To the willow tree you like so much." Laila smiled at her daughter. "The early morning rays will be the perfect light."

Kylin crinkled her nose then hiked up her gown as she walked in front of the willow. Her eyes squinted as she looked at the first rays of sun. Finally defeated, she let them pose her, move her hair around, reposition her dress, and carefully move her head for the best light.

"Kylin, you look beautiful."

"I'd better be after all of this."

Laila watched as a slight breeze played through her daughter's hair. "You will…and if you don't, I'm sure Aethelhard will love it."

Kylin bit her bottom lip trying hard not to say anything back.

After what seemed like forever, the basic portrait was completed. Kylin stood up from the bench she'd been sitting on this whole time and stretched. Before Marie could get her gown, Kylin hiked it up again not caring who saw her as she headed for the keep to get the corset off so she could breathe again.

Marie followed quickly after her finally catching the end of the gown. "Kylin, you mustn't expose your legs as such. Even if it's only early for you, many of the others are awake and starting their chores."

Kylin glanced back at Marie. "And I shouldn't be up before dawn."

Marie walked behind her keeping her gown from getting dirty.

At last…they were in Kylin's chambers. Before the door even closed, Kylin was trying to wriggle out of her dress.

"Wait Kylin, I'll help you."

"Just get this corset off of me!" Kylin was exasperated.

Marie took off her dress laying it carefully on a large chair then unlaced her corset.

Kylin breathed deeply. "Finally, I can breathe again." She waited for Marie to get the rest of her clothes off then snuggled under the warm furs again. By the time Marie had hung up all her wedding garments, Kylin was fast asleep.

She tiptoed to the door, then closed it quietly.

Soon Marie came down for a pot of mead and a cup.

"Kylin not coming down?"

"No, milady. She wanted to get some rest before she left her room."

Laila gently shook her head as she chuckled. "Kylin has much to learn yet."

"May I go to milady's room?"

Laila nodded as she took another sip of her hot mead knowing there was much to do today to prepare for the wedding.

Kylin came down in the early afternoon a cup of lukewarm mead in her hand.

"Feeling better now?"

Kylin put down her cup and poured another cup of hot mead. She nodded as she sat down just before her eyes flew open.

"Do you like it?"

Kylin shrugged her shoulders as she turned away from it. "I'm not used to seeing myself like that." She put a little honey in her mead, her eyes looking away. "Will that be hung up before the wedding?"

Laila got up from her chair. "Not until after the wedding." She headed for the kitchen to see how preparations were going.

Suddenly there was the sound of trumpets announcing the arrival of someone. Kylin closed her eyes hoping it was Aethelhard.

Marie ran inside the dining room. "Milady, Milord Aethelhard has arrived."

Kylin ran out the door toward the drawbridge. Squinting in the afternoon sun, she saw Aethelhard's form come into view. She waited until Aethelhard handed his steed over to the stable boys before walking to him.

"You were gone a long time."

He smiled as his dark green eyes smoldered. "I wanted to make sure I wasn't called back to the castle until after we are wed."

"Aethelhard, nice to see you back," Hutton said by the stable. "Come, I wanted to discuss parts of the wedding with you."

Aethelhard took Kylin's chin and raised it until she looked into his eyes. "Duty calls but I will see you soon." Kylin's heart quivered as she gazed into his eyes remembering their first kiss under the willow. As soon as he turned to meet up with Hutton, Kylin ran to the kitchen to find her mother. She wanted to marry him right now.

"Mother," she called out to the kitchen.

Laila spoke with the baker for a moment more then met Kylin. "What is it, my dear?"

"Aethelhard just arrived. How much longer will it take to prepare for the wedding?"

Laila laughed softly. "He arrived a day earlier than Hutton and I thought. It won't be long to finish preparations." She smiled at her daughter. "Get with Marie. Flower decorations and a garland must be made."

"Yes, Mother," Kylin said excited. "Marie, where are you?"

Marie's head popped up from the kitchen. "Here, milady."

"Come, we must get the flowers ready."

Kylin ran toward the garden she knew so well with Marie not too far behind. There were so many flowers in full bloom. They would be able to make beautiful arrangements for all the wedding.

They worked on the flowers most of the day until twilight.

Kylin yawned as she noticed the long rays of the sun were dipping down below the western horizon. "I didn't know it was so late."

"You must be exhausted," Marie said as she looked over the lilac bushes. "Milady Laila said the wedding would take place the day after tomorrow. We've time tomorrow to finish the flowers."

Kylin sighed softly. "It's difficult to believe I'll be marrying Aethelhard."

Marie smiled as she looked at Kylin. "You were meant to be together."

Kylin stood up from the bench, stretched, then walked down the path toward the dining area.

Chapter 9

Kylin awoke the next morning with bright rays of sunshine peeking through the tapestry which hung over her window. She stretched then looked out the small window.

"The flowers," she thought suddenly. She looked around for Marie but didn't find her anywhere in sight. She dressed herself then quickly opened the door almost causing Marie to spill the hot mead she was bringing to her.

"You are awake, milady. I was bringing hot mead for you."

"We need to finish the flowers today."

Marie handed the mead to Kylin. "There's time, milady."

Kylin sat down by the hearth and sipped her mead. "There's so much to do today."

Marie brushed Kylin's long hair. "We must first make you presentable. Sit back and drink your mead."

Kylin finished her mead as Marie brushed then braided her hair. "There! That should keep your hair nice and tidy today."

"Is Aethelhard awake?"

"Yes, but he's with Milord D'arcy. Come, let's finish the flowers."

Reluctantly, she rose to her feet. "I wish I could see Aethelhard."

"You'll see him soon enough. Milord D'arcy and Milord Elwyn are overseeing the unloading of the wagons."

Soon Kylin, Marie, and the other women Marie had recruited were back in the gardens making small flower bouquets that the guests could take home after the wedding. It was almost dark before Marie and Kylin started on her garland. Marie's hands were busy twisting and twining the fresh rosemary and roses into a garland for Kylin. "Fit for a princess," Marie said after placing it on her head. She took the wreath from Kylin's head then wove some ribbons from her pocket into the garland with the longer ribbons hanging so they would fall over her back.

"I never knew making so many bouquets would make me this tired." Kylin yawned.

"Go rest Milady. We can finish the bouquets ourselves."

Kylin entered the dining room taking some fresh fruit and bread along with a pot of hot mead to her chambers.

"I'll just lay down for a little while," she thought. She awoke during the night long enough to take her gown off and put her bedclothes on. She was soon fast asleep again.

She awoke to the early morning rays of light dancing around her chamber. With only her night clothes on, she ran to the small window and peaked outside to see all the activity. The word of their wedding spread rapidly through the village. The villagers in their best clothes were already milling about waiting for the wedding festivities to start.

"Come milady, it's time to shed your night clothes for your bath."

Kylin turned from the window and danced her way to Maria. "I wasn't happy for the first wedding you prepared me for but for this one, I can hardly wait. I can't believe I'll soon be Aethelhard's bride."

Maria smiled lifting her night dress off and laying it on the bed. "You are happier with this wedding." Maria held Kylin's hand as she stepped into the warm water. She sank into the warm perfumed water closing her eyes. She breathed deeply of the sweet rose oil. "Where did the oils come from?"

"They were some of the goods from the wagons that arrived yesterday," Marie said as she mixed herbs in a pitcher of warm water then unbraided Kylin's hair.

Kylin soaked in the warm water. "What are you making in the pitcher?"

"It's a blend of herbs for your hair."

"It smells nice. What herbs are in there?"

Marie smiled as she began to help Kylin bathe. "There's rosemary water, nettles, mint, thyme and a little vinegar to make your hair shine after it dries."

After Marie was satisfied that Kylin's skin smelled of roses, she helped Kylin stand in the tub then she poured the herb perfumed water over her hair. She ran her fingers through Kylin's hair making sure all her hair was bathed with the herb water. After drying her, Marie wrapped a warm blanket around her then started to comb her hair with an ivory comb.

"Where did you get the comb?" She assumed it was her mother's.

"Milord Elwyn bought it for you with an ivory brush and hand mirror."

Kylin smiled as Marie continued brushing her long hair until it was dry. Gently she pulled her hair back, so it lay just below her ears, then wove a fishtail braid so it lay down her back. She took some of the fresh flowers and wove those into the braid as well making sure her wedding garland would be seen from the front.

Maria finished helping her dress except for her gown. Kylin twisted as Marie laced her corset. "I still don't see why I have to wear this." She struggled to take a deep breath.

"Milady D'arcy insists." There was a gentle knock at the door and Marie answered it. "Everything is ready except for her dress."

"Thank you, Marie. I'll help her into her dress."

"Yes, milady," Marie said as she walked out and quietly closed the door.

"Your hair is beautiful. Marie always makes such pretty braids." Laila walked to Kylin's bed and picked up the gown. "I do love the pearls and cloak. I wanted to make sure you were warm. It still gets cool in the evening." The dress made of silk was dyed to a deep royal blue. The cloak made of the same royal blue as the silk dress. On the long sleeves were the pearls which ran down the outside of the gown's arm. Laila smiled as she helped Kylin into her dress. "You look lovely. Look in the mirror."

Kylin moved closer to the full-length mirror. She blinked a couple of times to make sure it was her she was looking at. She turned to look at the sides. Laila handed her the ivory hand mirror so she could see the braid Marie wove. "I don't look like myself at all," Kylin said softly.

Laila gave her a hug. "Every woman should look like a princess on her wedding day." She placed the cloak over Kylin's shoulders carefully to not disturb her braid and handed Kylin her garland.

"Come, it's time for your wedding," Laila took her daughter's hand. Once outside the keep, Hutton took Kylin's hand then Laila's hand and escorted them both to the church.

As soon as Kylin saw Aethelhard at the church, she her heart quivered. Aethelhard smiled to his beautiful bride. To him she looked like an angel. Hutton placed Kylin's hand into Aethelhard's hand then sat with Laila.

At the end of the wedding ceremony, Aethelhard placed Kylin's garland wreath on her head. He took her sapphire ring placing it on her left ring finger bringing her hand to his lips as he kissed the ring. "With the sealing of this ring, I proclaim to all that you are my wife. I also commit my love and protection to you always." Kylin looked up at him with tear in her eyes. He brought her closer and kissed her. He took her hand as everyone in the chapel clapped and led her down the aisle

As they were walking down the church isle, Kylin paused briefly thinking she saw her mother's sister Dalila but was quickly led out of the church by Aethelhard. Dalila was her aunt, but she seldom left the Hy-Brasil island. Maybe it was just the tears of joy blurring her vision.

Kylin heard the loud clash of the joust starting. Aethelhard lead her to their place in the box, nodding to her. "Milady Elwyn, your seat." He smiled as she sat down. It was music to his ears to be the first to address her with her new surname.

After the jousting, Hutton called from the entrance of the dining area. "Come, the feast is ready."

Kylin and Aethelhard walked with the crowd to the dining area. Once inside she took her seat with Aethelhard at the long table reserved for the bride, groom, and their respective families.

Hutton raised his cup with the mead. "A toast to Kylin and Aethelhard. May they always be as happy as they are today." Everyone raised their cups with many of the crowd saying, "Here, here".

Every table was loaded with fresh baked bread and various types of cheeses. Large bowls were filled with eggs, mutton, venison, chicken, duck, salmon, and hare. Sweet tarts, pastries, and honeyed breads were also abundant. Several bottles of mead were on the tables as well. Soon after the toast everyone was loading their plate with the feast before them. Kylin shortly excused herself.

Aethelhard looked to her puzzled. "Do you feel faint?"

She shook her head and whispered. "I'll be right back."

She crept to the cellar just inside the kitchen and stepped down the creaking stairs. Hopefully, no one would be down for a while. She struggled and struggled not able to rid herself of that retched thing. Finally, her fingers found the tie. She pulled hard, the tie came undone, and she wriggled out of it. She tossed it behind some large barrels and took a deep breath. Now she was ready to feast. She ran up the stairs making sure no one saw her emerge then to the dining room smiling as she sat next to Aethelhard.

There was much entertainment, food, and mead. Every so often, Kylin looked over the crowded dining room to see if she could find Dalila. She must have come only for the wedding ceremony then left for the island. Aethelhard took Kylin's hands to dance with her as the music started.

It was into the early morning hours when Aethelhard took Kylin's hand and quietly lead her away. Once away from the activity, he lifted her as he carried her to his chamber.

A year later Nantres was born. Talk about how Aethelhard felt after knowing his mother and sister died. The trembling as he thought he would now lose Kylin and their son. He wasn't allowed into the room but stood outside the door praying; never leaving. How Kylin's screams scared him. He trembled hearing the screams of his mother while she was giving birth…then the dreadful silence as the baby never cried…never took a breath.

Then the relief when the midwife gently caught him and saying what a healthy baby he is. His skin is so pink and his crying loud. Yes, he was a healthy one. Aethelhard enters the room smiling at his wriggling baby. He looked a Kylin then to his baby boy. His name will be Nantres. In her exhaustion Kylin whispers Nantres as the midwife sets him on her chest. Dalila knows as well. Kylin has delivered a healthy baby boy. A tear slips down her cheek as she couldn't be there for her grandson's birth. Vassago and his demons were watching her every move. He knew something important to Dalila was to happen soon. She didn't dare be there for the birth as she didn't know if her grandson was human as his mother or more like her and Laila. She does the only thing she can…she blesses him.

Chapter 10

Nantres was excited for his fifth birthday especially since his grandmother said she had a surprise. Nantres waited in the castle tower for Hutton and Laila to arrive for his birthday. Laila told him this would be a special day. The knight nudged Nantres as their horses came into view. Nantres' eyes opened wide and he ran down the stairs to greet them.

Aethelhard and Kylin were coming out of the keep as Nantres ran to be with his grandparents. He reached his arms to his grandmother as she dismounted, and she hugged him tightly.

"I remembered what you told me," Nantres said to his grandmother. "I'm ready."

Laila looked to Hutton then smiled to him. "Are you sure?"

Nantres nodded his head quickly. "I've been waiting for this special day."

Laila smiled. "I need to talk with your mother and father for a few minutes, then we'll go for a walk. Go with your grandfather and show him how well you're doing with your sword."

Nantres hugged her. "Will you be talking very long?"

"Not long," Laila answered.

Nantres and Hutton walked toward the squires so Nantres could show him what he had learned.

Kylin looked curiously at her mother. "What did you have to tell us that Nantres couldn't hear?"

Laila walked with them into the keep and closed the door. "He'll find out soon all he needs to know. I've seen Nantres shows much promise. His skills with the sword and knowledge are already advanced for his age."

Aethelhard smiled proudly taking Kylin's hand. "He's been doing well with both."

Laila looked to them. "I didn't want to tell you until I was sure. Enough time has passed."

"Tell us what, mother?" Kylin asked.

"You have heard of the excubant in custodiis crucis?"

"Of course," Kylin said. "They are magical and keepers of the cross. It is said the cross comes from the magical island of Hy-Brasil."

"I'm an excubant in custodiis crucis," Laila said.

Kylin's eyes grew large. "You are? But why didn't you tell me until now?"

"Because you did not show the magical traits of the excubant in custodiis crucis, Kylin. However, Nantres does." Laila walked to a small table and sat down. "Come, there's much for me to tell both of you. Kylin, you aren't my and Hutton's daughter even though we always loved you as a daughter."

"Whose daughter am I then?"

"You are my sister, Dalila, and Vassago's daughter."

"Who's Vassago?"

"Kylin, let me finish telling you everything then you can ask questions. It will make it easier for all of us. Vassago is a demon but a good-natured demon. Dalila brought you here to keep you safe. You weren't born with magic and she didn't want any harm to come to you by the demons. They don't usually bother young children, but she couldn't take any chances. It has been told to us long ago that another would come to take the cross and bring peace to our lands and England. The magic came through you by having Nantres. We believe he's the one who will bring peace to our lands and banish the demons further away so they will not bother anyone who lives on Hy-Brasil. Two of Vassago's powers are to make women fall in love with him and finding things. Vassago seduced Dalila. Soon after, she was pregnant with you."

Laila took a drink of her water and continued. "Did you see Dalila at your wedding?"

"I thought I saw her. It was a brief glance then she was gone."

"Dalila was able to make it to your wedding, unfortunately, she couldn't be here for Nantres' birth. Vassago found out she had a child and had his demons following her every step. She wanted so much to see her grandson born but it would have been too big of a risk to be here. However, while Dalila was here for the wedding, she gave me the cross for safe keeping. She was able to trick Vassago into telling her where he'd hid the cross just before she left the island. As soon as I could, I brought it to the chapel and gave it to the priest. He would be able to keep it hidden until the cross could be unveiled. I'm pretty sure that's what Claec's imposter was looking for as well. I've watched Nantres grow and I believe he is the one we have been waiting for."

"You have the cross?" Kylin asked surprised.

Laila pulled the necklace chain up so they could see the cross. She then tucked it back into the bodice of her dress. "Yes. The cross will tell us if Nantres is the one. Today he turns five. This is the day all of us will find out if he will truly be the keeper of the cross. That's also why there are so many tunnels around the Nottes. It's to keep the cross safe. It has been back and forth to both castles to make sure Vassago wouldn't find it. The priest, a man of God, was able to keep Vassago from finding it."

"Why did you leave Hy-Brasil?", Kylin asked."

"We can get off and, on the island, if we choose. Most who are born there, stay. It's quite beautiful. I left for what I thought would be only a few weeks, but I met Hutton at a Faire. I kept delaying going back to Hy-Brasil because I fell in love him. I wasn't sure if Morgana would approve of him living at Hy-Brasil. Morgana has the island cloaked in mist to protect King Arthur's grave and body. He's her brother. If it can't be found by those who were born off the island, his grave will stay safe. There are many who are looking for his sword, Excalibur. It holds great magic."

"Is Excalibur on the island?"

Laila smiled to her son-in-law. "Only Morgana can answer that question."

"Does Morgana live on the island?" asked Aethelhard.

"She spends most of her time across the great stream although, she does come back now and then to make sure King Arthur's grave hasn't been disturbed."

"What about Vassago?" Kylin asked curiously.

Laila sat back in her chair. "They live on the north side of the island just past Morgana. The fairies and those of good magic live on the south part of the island. The north and south part of Hy-Brasil are separated by the great stream. Vassago is more mischievous than evil. He can be quite helpful at times. Morgana allows him to live there but he must keep his demons from those of good heart. She was very angry when she found that Vassago had impregnated Dalila. It's for that reason Vassago and his demons now live underwater. The part of the island north of Morgana was sunk deep into the sea to make it more difficult for him to get to the south part of the island without being seen."

"And the magic?" Kylin questioned.

Laila shifted in her chair, her eyes growing distant as she remembered all those years ago. "Aethelhard, do you remember when you were running with Kylin and I found you? I was in a wagon. I had gray hair and drawn skin."

Aethelhard looked to her curiously. "Yes. At first, I didn't think it was you until I heard your voice. I'd often wondered how you did that."

"There was also a key that you found while the Claec imposter held you prisoner."

"Yes," Aethelhard said thinking back. "I also remember when I was trying to find the passageway into Nottes Castle keep. I saw a light in my mind. It showed me where the stones to push were."

Laila nodded. "I did all of those things. I disguised myself to get you safely into the castle, brought the key to you when you were held prisoner, and showed you where the stones were to the passageway. That's part of my magic and that's the magic I believe Nantres holds as well." Laila looked to the door. "Now it's time to see if Nantres truly holds the magic."

Kylin hugged her mother. "And if he is Custodem Saltus Crucis?"

"Dalila and I will teach Nantres of his magic. Dalila will be here as much as she can. I'll make sure you how to keep him safe. The cross will be hidden until he's ready to receive it," Laila said softly.

Kylin released her mother. "Why must the cross be hidden at all times?"

"There is much magic in the cross especially when it joins with two swords. If someone of good heart has it, there will be peace on the earth." Laila pursed her lips and closed her eyes. Her eyes flickered open and she took a deep breath. "If someone of evil possesses the cross and two swords, he or she will have the power to destroy all of earth including Hy-Brasil."

Kylin looked to Aethelhard then nodded in understanding. Laila opened the door and walked over to where Nantres was playing. As soon as he saw her, he ran to her.

"Now?" Nantres said excited.

Laila reached for his hand and nodded. "Now."

Laila and Nantres walked up the hill, the wind rushing over them, whispering to Nantres. He stopped as they neared the top of the hill.

"Why are you stopping?"

He turned his head smiling. "They are speaking to me."

"Who is speaking to you?"

"The spirits. They talk to me sometimes," Nantres said innocently.

"What are they telling you now?"

"Not to be afraid," he said distantly while listening.

They walked out over a ledge that jutted from the hill. "Nantres, in time, you will come to discover the magic that is from the spirits as well. You should never be afraid of them for it is part of who you are."

Nantres listened understanding even at his early age.

Laila reached down to pick up Nantres as they stood on the ledge. "One day all of the magic will be yours as well, Nantres. You must learn to control it and never let it control you." She reached around her neck, taking the cross necklace off and slowly placing it around Nantres' neck. "Remember the spirits telling you not to be afraid?"

Nantres nodded, his tiny fingers moving over the metal cross as it started to glow. Lightning raced across the sky and the wind blew around them, blessing the union of child and cross.